We Wish You a Messy Christmas

BOOKS BY MELODY CARLSON

HOLIDAY NOVELLAS

Once Upon a Christmas Carol
The Christmas Tree Farm
A Royal Christmas
The Christmas Quilt
Christmas in the Alps
The Christmas Swap
Christmas in Winter Hill
A Christmas by the Sea
The Christmas Blessing
The Christmas Angel Project
The Christmas Joy Ride
The Christmas Cat
A Simple Christmas Wish
The Christmas Pony
The Treasure of Christmas
The Joy of Christmas
The Christmas Shoppe
Christmas at Harrington's

CONTEMPORARY ROMANCE

All Booked Up
Welcome to the Honey B&B
Just for the Summer
Second Time Around
Looking for Leroy
The Happy Camper
Courting Mr. Emerson

FOLLOW YOUR HEART SERIES

Under a Summer Sky
All Summer Long
Once Upon a Summertime

We Wish You a Messy Christmas

A Holiday Novella

MELODY CARLSON

Revell
a division of Baker Publishing Group
Grand Rapids, Michigan

Published by Revell
a division of Baker Publishing Group
Grand Rapids, Michigan
RevellBooks.com

Printed in the United States of America

Library of Congress Cataloging-in-Publication Data
Names: Carlson, Melody author
Title: We wish you a messy Christmas : a holiday novella / Melody Carlson.
Description: Grand Rapids, Michigan : Revell, a division of Baker Publishing Group, 2026.
Identifiers: LCCN 2025048653 | ISBN 9780800747671 cloth | ISBN 9781493455522 ebook
Subjects: LCGFT: Christmas fiction | Christian fiction | Novellas
Classification: LCC PS3553.A73257 W43 2026
LC record available at https://lccn.loc.gov/2025048653

This book is a work of fiction. Names, characters, places, and incidents are the product of the author's imagination or are used fictitiously. Any resemblance to actual events, locales, or persons, living or dead, is coincidental.

Illustration by Nate Eidenberger
Cover design by Laura Klynstra

Baker Publishing Group publications use paper produced from sustainable forestry practices and postconsumer waste whenever possible.

26 27 28 29 30 31 32   7 6 5 4 3 2 1

one

OLIVIA BRADSHAW RELEASED a loud groan as she dropped her shopping bags inside the apartment. "Why do I keep doing this?" she muttered to herself as she peeled off her coat and unwound her wool scarf, shaking the rain onto the tiled entryway floor.

"Keep doing what?" her roommate Tracie asked from behind her. "And why are you talking to yourself?"

"Oh, was I?" Olivia kicked off her soggy shoes. "I thought you were going out to hunt down a Christmas tree."

"That was the plan, but Josh canceled. Due to weather." Tracie peered curiously at her. "Is something wrong?"

"You're the shrink." Olivia wrinkled her nose. "You tell me."

"First of all, I dislike the word *shrink*. Next of all, I'm only an intern until I get my license next summer." She pointed to the sofa. "But if you'd like to talk, I'm a pretty good listener. Not going anywhere this weekend."

Olivia frowned out the window. "Yeah, it's a deluge out there. Not supposed to let up for several days." She turned and sank into the sofa with a loud sigh.

"So, tell me, what's up?" Tracie shoved a throw pillow behind her and leaned back.

"I'm not totally sure I can explain it." Olivia pursed her lips. "But don't they say that repeating the same behavior and expecting a different outcome is the definition of insanity?"

"Then be comforted, you're in good company." Tracie smiled. "So what is it you keep doing with unsurprising results?"

Olivia studied her roommate. They'd been friends for less than a year and roommates only since summer. Tracie seemed so put together and intelligent that Olivia was reluctant to spill the beans about her weird family. Make that her weird *mother*. In Dad's defense, he was pretty normal. An enabler perhaps, but basically a good guy. Still, Tracie had never met Olivia's parents or visited their home.

Tracie nodded toward the heap of bags piled by the door. "Looks like you scored with your shopping excursion. Is your problem perhaps overspending? Lots of people do that this time of year. Not too late to return things."

"Thankfully, that's not necessary. In fact, shopping, despite the lousy weather, was fun. This is my first year buying real Christmas presents for everyone and, okay, I might've gone overboard, but thanks to my raise from the marketing firm, I didn't need to charge a single thing this year. That's not why I'm bummed."

"Is this related to Malcolm?"

"No, not exactly. I mean, we're okay. Really, Malcolm is great." Olivia twisted her mouth to one side. To be honest, her mixed feelings were slightly related to Malcolm. Not directly, but partly. Anyway, Malcolm could complicate things.

Tracie held up her hands like she was ready to give up. "Okay then, if you don't want to talk—"

"I do want to talk," Olivia burst out. "I *need* to talk. It's just hard to explain. I don't know where to begin. And I'm probably making a mountain out of a molehill."

"Go ahead, start digging." Tracie leaned back again.

"Well, it's about my mom. And already, I feel like a spoiled brat to whine about it."

"Spoiled brat? Why?"

"For talking smack about my mom. For being ungrateful, for taking her for granted . . ."

"Uh-huh? How's that?"

"Because, well, because my mom is perfect. Jane Bradshaw is absolute perfection."

"Perfection . . . ?" Tracie's brow creased. "And that's a bad thing?"

"See why I feel like the ungrateful daughter?" Olivia was aware that Tracie had been born into severe dysfunction, followed by foster care and finally adoption to the family she now recognized as her own. And yet she seemed so unscathed by it all. "I hate hearing myself complain about my mom."

Tracie held up one hand. "Okay, let's make this a judgment-free zone."

"Yeah . . . right."

"So, can you describe to me how your mom is, uh, *perfect*?"

"It's everything. The way she acts, her manners and mannerisms. The way she looks—she's an impeccable dresser who seems to wake up with perfect hair and makeup. The way she keeps her home immaculate and organized. Honestly, this woman is so meticulous, she could probably cook and clean and decorate the pants off Martha Stewart."

Tracie laughed. "I'd like to see that."

"But I feel guilty saying all this. My mom's always been my

number one supporter. You know, the kind of mother who has warm homemade cookies waiting after school, clean laundry folded and put away in your room. She knits and sews and even used to sew me dresses when I was little."

"Sounds like *Donna Reed*—remember that old sitcom?"

Olivia shook her head but continued. "I'm an only child, and Mom's always been there for me. I know I should be grateful." Olivia cringed. "But she really makes me crazy. I used to imagine she came from another planet. Like a robot or Stepford wife. Have you ever seen that movie?"

Tracie nodded. "Okay, I get that. Sounds like a lot to grow up with. But I've never seen you get upset about it before. Did something trigger you today? How did she get under your skin right now?"

"It started with Malcolm. We met for coffee this morning, and he started to talk about Christmas. He's taking vacation time and was so excited about going home and seeing everyone." Olivia felt a fresh wave of angst. "I told you how we grew up in the same town, went to the same school, lived in the same neighborhood."

"Yeah. I love how you guys just chance-met after years. Sweet serendipity when you picked up your associate's cat from the vet clinic several months ago."

"Yeah, I'd heard Malcolm had his veterinarian degree but had no idea he practiced here in Salem."

"I call it a God wink."

"Yup. And so far, it's been amazing. But now that we both plan to go home for Christmas . . . well, that's where it gets dicey."

"How so?"

"My parents still live near Malcolm's parents. Right next door, in fact."

"Sounds pretty convenient. Maybe you can combine your Christmas celebrations."

"Think again. The ugly truth is that my mother cannot stand the McEntires. Last I heard, she won't even speak to Cindy."

"Oh?" Tracie's brows arched. "So maybe your mom isn't so perfect after all."

Olivia solemnly nodded.

"And I'm guessing your relationship with Malcolm could be problematic for both your families during the holidays."

"Like a Romeo and Juliet horror film."

Tracie leaned forward. "And your parents don't know about you and Malcolm?"

"They have no idea." Olivia bit her lower lip. "And everything has been so amazingly magical with Malcolm . . . I just don't want to see it ruined. Especially at Christmastime. It might be premature, or just my hopeful imagining, but I think he's dropping some hints. I have a feeling he might be thinking marriage. Can you imagine how awkward an engagement ring for Christmas could become for our families?"

"If Malcolm did propose, would you accept?"

"I wish I could say yes, but to be honest, I don't know. I mean, I love Malcolm, but I love my parents too. I don't want to be estranged from them. I've seen friends caught in the center of parental dramas before. Not pretty. Families can really impact a marriage . . . and with kids, well, it's even more complicated."

"Yeah. I know. So, is there a reason for this family feud?

Something that could somehow be repaired? Maybe you and Malcolm are meant to be the catalyst here."

"Maybe . . . and I realize a catalyst can get things moving, but it can also blow things to pieces." Olivia forced an uneasy smile, thinking the latter was probably more likely. This year could be a very messy Christmas.

two

JANE BRADSHAW PACED back and forth past her living room front window, biting her lower lip and twisting a dust cloth in her hands, trying to appear nonchalant as she peered outside to the chaos next door. She hated it when Rob called her Mrs. Kravitz after the snoopy neighbor on the old *Bewitched* sitcom. And she knew it was ridiculous, bordering on obsessive, to get this worked up over a silly birthday party. But for some unexplainable reason, this felt like the proverbial writing on the wall. Things were not going to get better.

Her next-door neighbor and "friendly" nemesis, Cindy McEntire, was celebrating turning sixty today. And good for her, but was that milestone really worthy of all this fuss? But then Cindy had about a dozen grown children and probably twice as many grandchildren, and their property currently resembled a junkyard on steroids. Besides the gaudy signs, streamers, and balloons littered recklessly about and getting soaked in the afternoon rain, cars in various conditions were crammed everywhere in the cul-de-sac, which was rather short on parking. And like adding insult to injury, Rob had invited the guests to use the Bradshaw driveway for overflow parking. And it had overflowed right into their planting strip.

"Rob!" she called out for the third time, ready to lash into her husband over his lapse in good sense. "Come here right this minute."

Rob slowly ambled into the room with a small gift bag in hand. "What's wrong?" he asked with a furrowed brow. "Is the house on fire? I don't hear any alarms."

"Look at that." She pointed out the window to their driveway. "That vehicle's tires are in our planting strip."

"Yeah, I know. But it's not on the shrubbery or hurting anything. Not that you should care since you've been nagging me to clear out that juniper anyway."

"Not like that." She frowned. "And what if I need to get my car out of the garage? I'm totally blocked in."

"You said you didn't feel well and didn't plan on going anywhere today. Including Cindy's birthday party." He held the bag up. "I was about to go."

"You are actually going over there?"

"Why not? Erik invited us last week. And they're our neighbors. And they're good people."

"They're a train wreck."

His mouth twisted to one side. "We're all entitled to our opinions. And we've agreed to disagree on this." He gave her his warning look, a signal that he was done with this conversation. "And no worries, Jane, I made your excuses this morning. Not that Erik believed it when I said you have a headache."

Jane touched her forehead. "Maybe I didn't have one then, but I'm getting one now." She stared at the cheerful bag he'd obviously snuck from her crafting room. "What's in there?"

"Just something for Cindy's birthday."

She stepped closer, trying to peer into the bag. "What is it?"

He sheepishly removed a chunky coffee mug in garish colors, turning it toward her so she could see the words. "Found it at that little doodad shop next door to my office."

"'May your coffee kick in before reality does,'" she read aloud, then grimly shook her head. "I wish reality *would* kick in—and maybe kick her right in the—"

"Jane," he chided, "that's no way to love thy neighbor. And on her birthday too."

She closed her eyes and blew out a sigh. "I know, I know. I'm a terrible Christian. But can I help it if Cindy McEntire drives me absolutely nuts? I honestly thought with their menagerie of kids all grown, their house would quiet down some. But now that they're getting married and bearing offspring, that place is a three-ring circus."

"A circus is a happy place." He attempted a smile.

"Not if the wild lions and tigers roam freely and do their business on your front lawn."

"Oh, Jane." He tucked the mug back in the bag, shoving some tissue paper on top. "Sure you don't want to go over there with me and wish her happy birthday? Erik said Jocelyn made carrot cake."

"No, thank you very much."

With a glum expression, he reached for his fleece jacket that was hanging on the antique hall tree by the front door, probably still dripping wet from when he went out earlier in the rain. How many times had she told him to hang wet things in the laundry room?

"I'll share your regards with Cindy," he said.

"Don't bother. I'm sure she wouldn't believe you anyway."

"Sure she would. Cindy has a very gracious spirit."

"You mean unlike *some* people," she said sharply.

"I never said that."

"You didn't need to." She felt guilty now. Why was she such a wet blanket? "I'm sorry, Rob. I don't mean to be so negative. But all those cars and those soggy birthday decorations, well, I guess they just put me on edge."

"They'll be gone soon enough. I'll help Erik take them down."

"Yeah, then they'll be replaced with their usual tacky Christmas decorations. I'm surprised they're not already up." She felt a twinge of hope. "Maybe they'll back off this year."

"Erik said they both were down with the flu right after Thanksgiving." He reached for the door.

"Probably one of their lovely grandchildren shared a bug with them," she said. "You be careful over there, Rob. It might still be going around." She followed him to the door. "And be sure to wash your hands. And for heaven's sake, don't eat anything. I've been in that woman's kitchen."

He just laughed. "Yeah, yeah, you've mentioned that before. But everyone knows you're a germaphobe, Jane. No one's housekeeping will ever measure up to yours." He pecked her on the cheek. "Have a nice afternoon."

She refrained from a juvenile eye roll. But honestly, did he really expect her to have a nice afternoon with that chaotic, noisy mob next door? She closed and locked the door behind him and let out an involuntary shudder. Turning to the hall, she stared at her image in the oval mirror. The old beveled looking glass was somewhat fogged with age, and the overcast skies outside made the foyer seem dimmer, but her image seemed extra dark. Was it her imagination? Or did she really look that dark and gloomy?

She'd always been considered an attractive person. Even though her hair had turned prematurely white in her early forties, it had remained thick, and she kept it cut in a youthful bob. Although it did seem limp and dull today. Probably time to put the special blue rinse on it to give it the sparkle and shine that always gained her compliments. And Rob used to say her eyes were as blue as the ocean on a clear day, but they looked pale and rather grayish today. And were those new wrinkles? She leaned closer to see. Was it just her imagination? Or was she turning into an ugly old woman with a truly bad disposition? And if so, how did it happen?

Jane kept staring at the grumpy woman in the mirror, scowling and making ugly faces, wondering if this was how she appeared to others. She didn't want to be like this. Besides being unbecoming, her grisly expression seemed to accentuate the wrinkles that had shown up uninvited lately. Was it already time for Botox again? She attempted a smile, hoping to appear more youthful, but it simply looked phony. Like her. She knew she was a phony, always trying to appear to have it together, wearing the perfect clothes, living in the perfect home, saying the perfect things . . . when she was really crumbling on the inside. And yet she felt helpless, trapped in the prison she'd built for herself. Besides being a killjoy and wet blanket to people like the McEntires, she was also turning into a cranky old fishwife. Amazing that Rob could even stand her.

She turned away from the mirror and looked around her house. As usual, it was all perfection, and, in its perfection, it was soothing. She walked through the living room, straightening a pale blue pillow on the sofa, picking a fading leaf from her philodendron, refolding a cream-colored chenille afghan, laying it perfectly over the cream-colored ottoman that matched the sofa. This room, all in pale blues and shades of white, was relatively easy to keep perfect since Rob rarely came in here. His domain was his man cave–like den, which probably needed her touch right now.

She headed in that direction. It always got away from her a bit on the weekends since Rob used it more, but to her surprise, it was fairly neat. She straightened his stack of golf and fitness magazines before picking up his slippers and carrying them to their bedroom, where she put them in his closet. As usual, his walk-in closet was a bit chaotic, but after too many arguments over her "infringing on his territory," she had learned to kick a path on the cluttered floor, hang up his clean, pressed shirts, close the door, and look the other way. She was halfway tempted to straighten it all up now—just out of spite. But she didn't think it would be worth the fight.

You'd think a man with his own accounting firm would want to keep things at home as neat and tidy as he kept the books for the biggest businesses in town. But left to his own ways, Rob would be a total mess. Would he be happier in his filth? Perhaps. But she couldn't go there. She didn't even know the way.

three

THERE WAS ONLY a cold drizzle when Olivia walked to the coffeehouse just a few blocks down from her apartment, but she felt like a soggy sponge halfway there. By the time she stepped inside, welcomed by the scent of freshly ground coffee beans, she was dripping. Malcolm waved from a table right next to the woodstove, and, relieved for some warmth and dry heat, she peeled off her damp jacket and joined him.

"I'm really starting to hate city living," she admitted as she sat down.

"Well, I heard it's raining at home too," he consoled her.

"Yeah, but temps are supposed to go down next week, and it sounds like they might start getting snow there." She sighed and unpeeled a damp woolen scarf. "I'd take that over this any day." She smiled as a barista set down a latte with a pretty heart cut into the foam. Malcolm obviously knew the way to her heart. "Thanks." She carefully picked up the mug, feeling the warmth seep into her fingers. "So, why were you checking the weather at home?"

"I wasn't. Jocelyn called and reminded me it's Mom's birthday."

"Oh?"

"Yeah, her sixtieth. And they're having a big blowout birthday bash today. An all-day and overnight get together. Mom's over the moon."

Olivia nodded. "She loves celebrations like that."

"Mostly having her family gathered around." His cheerful countenance faded some.

"And you should be there too?" She sipped her latte, savoring the mellow sweetness of the vanilla and sprinkle of sugar that had been added.

"Yeah. I totally forgot."

"Are you on call at the clinic?"

"Not this weekend."

"Then you should go home, Malcolm." She checked the oversized clock on the wall. "Just think, you could be there by dinnertime if you left now."

"Yeah, I was just thinking that too." He pressed his lips tightly together, as if making a decision. "It's a two-hour drive . . . think you'd want to come along? I'm sure your parents would love a surprise visit from you."

She considered this. Maybe it'd be a good way to introduce her mom to the news that she was dating Malcolm McEntire and they were maybe getting serious.

"Yeah," she said slowly. "My parents would probably love that."

He looked intently into her eyes. "I'd like my parents to know that we've been seeing each other. But I know how you wanted to wait."

She bit her lip. "Maybe that's a good idea, to sort of clue

them in. Better than springing it on them at Christmas. Might give them a little time to adjust to the idea."

"I know you're nervous, Livvie, but if it's any consolation, my family already loves you. It's like you've been part of our family for ages."

She looked at him. This was the most they'd talked about their relationship and how it might impact their families. Did this mean he felt as serious as she did? Not that she wanted to push him on it, but she could hint.

"I guess I've been putting it off, Malcolm . . . well, you know . . . in case we stopped seeing each other."

His brow creased. "Meaning you're thinking about that? Because if you are, I hope you'll let me in on it. I got ghosted once before a few years ago and it was pretty miserable."

She beamed at him. "No, no, not at all. I suppose I'm worried about you doing that to me."

He reached for her hand, which was still slightly cold, and, cupping it in both hands, seemed to study her. "I've never been happier with anyone, Livvie. But if you plan to break my heart, I'd prefer to get it over with."

She shook her head no and they both smiled. For what felt like several minutes, they just gazed at each other, and she almost thought this could be the big moment, but then he looked at the clock.

"Hey, why don't I get to-go cups, and we'll be on our way. I don't need to pack a bag since Mom never throws anything away and I still have some random clothes and things there—and we'll be coming back here Sunday afternoon anyway. But you probably need to stop by your apartment. My car's outside. I'll take you by."

"Don't bother. I don't need to pack anything either. My

room is just how I left it and I've got stuff there. Let's just hit the road, Jack."

Once they had their to-go cups in hand, they walked the short distance to the car, and before long, Malcolm was navigating city traffic to the interstate. With her still-damp jacket in the backseat, Olivia utilized a car blanket like a shawl and, once the heater was cranked up, was cozy and warm.

"There might be snow on the pass," she pointed out as Malcolm turned onto the eastbound highway toward home.

"I figured, but I have my winter tires on. No worries."

"I can't believe Christmas is less than three weeks off." She plugged his charging cord into her nearly dead phone, wondering if she should give her mom a little heads-up text . . . except that might just send poor Mom into an unnecessary cleaning frenzy. Maybe a surprise was better.

"This is actually perfect timing for something else," he said mysteriously.

"Something else?" Her engagement radar perked up.

"Yeah. You know Dr. Wheeler and his veterinary practice? Well, I heard through my brother that he's talking about retirement and needs to hire an associate."

"Really?" She turned to stare at him. "Are you thinking about it? Seriously? I mean, moving back home?"

"It sounds like a great opportunity. I've always wanted a practice that treated some large animals too. I get tired of highly strung little yippy trophy dogs and spoiled, overfed old cats."

"That does sound a little pathetic."

"I don't want to forget everything I learned in school about treating large animals. And working alongside Doc Wheeler would be a fantastic opportunity."

She glumly nodded. "Yeah, but I would miss you."

For a long moment the only sound was the wiper blades going back and forth.

"You always say you'd never move back there, but do you really mean it?" he asked.

"I think I used to mean it, and then to be honest, it probably just became a habit. It's easy to say when you're trying to fit into big-city life. But I suppose I do miss it." She considered this. "But to be honest, it would be a challenge to live in the same town as my parents. More specifically, my mom. You know she can be sort of difficult."

He chuckled. "I know she can be a little finicky about some things."

"Some things? She's finicky about *everything*. The truth is, going home even for just an overnighter kinda sets my teeth on edge."

"But you said you plan to be home for the holidays," he reminded her.

"Yeah, I suppose this visit can be like a little booster shot to inoculate me for what's coming at me in a couple weeks." She attempted a lighthearted laugh.

"Your mom is going to be thrilled to see you."

"Malcolm," she began carefully, "do you think . . . I'm being totally serious now, but do you think my mom is, uh, normal?"

"Normal? Frankly, I don't know anyone who is normal, so I have no idea."

"Okay, okay. I realize there is no normal. But sometimes I worry that my mom has mental health issues. It's like she's in this perfectionist trap of her own making, and the older she gets, the worse it gets."

"Maybe it just seems that way since you're living away from

home. If you were around her all the time, you might not even notice. I mean, my family has a lot of weirdness. Like, Jocelyn is on this crazy minimalist kick. And Jonathon has ups and downs and—"

"Yeah, yeah, I know your family, and sure, they have their quirks, which I find rather uniquely charming. But my mom goes beyond that. According to Tracie, any behavior that negatively affects your life or those around you might be more than just an eccentric personality trait."

"Well, some people think my mom is a hoarder since her house is so packed. Do you think she has an issue?"

"I remember your mom's garage and yard sales. Seems she was always trying to thin out stuff. Doesn't strike me as hoarding. And after raising eight kids, it's no wonder she gets stuck with a lot of stuff. And they've been in that house for years and—"

"Okay, okay. Good defense. Maybe you should quit being a marketing consultant and take up law." He glanced her way. "Speaking of your career, I've heard that a lot of consultants work off-site, from home. Have you ever thought of that?"

"I do work off-site sometimes." She turned to look at him, studying his profile as he focused on the highway. "What made you think of that?"

He shrugged, then smiled. "I don't know." He pointed up the road to a pull-out next to the river. "I want to stop and take off my coat. I'm getting too warm."

"Yeah, and it stopped raining."

Malcolm slowed the car to a stop before getting out. Still wearing the blanket shawl, Olivia got out, too, going over to the guardrail to peer down at the raging river below.

"Pretty wild today," she said.

"Extreme kayakers might like it, but I'll take the calmer stuff." Malcolm unzipped his wool jacket and tossed it in the back. "Olivia," he said suddenly with a slightly urgent tone. "I hope that if I were to get a job with Doc Wheeler and relocate, we'd . . . uh, well, we'd still stay in touch, right?"

She nodded and smiled. "Of course." But even as she said it, she wondered . . . what did he actually mean? Stay in touch as in "let's remain friends"? Or continue with a long-distance dating relationship? Which honestly sounded unappealing. The distance part anyway. What was he really saying? She wanted to know and yet didn't want to ask. Didn't want to be an anchor holding him back from a dream.

He leaned over and gave her a quick kiss. "Because I don't want to lose this—whatever it is we have going on here." His smile filled her with a warm rush of assurance. And yet . . . what was he not saying?

"I don't want to lose it either." In that same instant, the heavy dark clouds overhead opened up again, and they both scrambled back to the SUV. *Okay*, she thought, *it wasn't the perfect spot for a marriage proposal. After all, who wants to say yes in the cold rain?* Although she had wished that was the moment, was ready for that to be the moment, and she would've eagerly said yes even while getting soaked to the skin. But it was probably for the best, since catching her parents off-guard by showing up unexpectedly combined with the news of an engagement . . . well, it might send her poor mother into cardiac arrest. Even a careful, albeit late-in-coming hint that romance was brewing would be more than enough to unhinge her mother. Not for the first time, Olivia wished she'd given her mom a little heads-up months ago when this was all fresh and new. What had she been waiting for anyway? Christmas?

four

AS ROB WENT for seconds at the loaded dining room table, every imaginable dish seemed to be there, from sushi to gnocchi to kimchi—an international smorgasbord. But since his taste was relatively tame, and since his wife rarely made it, he went for more lasagna. He knew Jane would give him hecky pecky, as his mother used to call it, for overeating so much rich food, and perhaps he'd pay for it at bedtime, but he did have a secret stash of Tums in his nightstand.

Pausing in the kitchen, fascinated by the chaotic clutter everywhere, he wondered if it was possible to love your wife for thirty-seven years and still not understand her. Rob didn't know the answer to that perplexity, and he'd been asking that question of himself for many years. Jane remained a mystery. She had a sweet, caring side and a critical, judgmental side. How did both of those personalities occupy the same woman? And, unless he was imagining things, her obsession with perfection was increasing with each passing year.

To be fair, he'd appreciated her commitment to homemaking early in the game. Their house was always immaculate, his clothes clean and pressed, good food on the table, their only child conscientiously parented. Some of his friends thought Jane was the ideal wife. Especially when so many of his friends had wives with their own demanding careers, Rob had felt lucky to have a stay-at-home wife. But then Olivia had gone off to college, and Jane had suddenly seemed more driven than ever. A friend had said it was just empty-nest syndrome, and she would mellow in time, but it seemed like her previous high standards had become more ramped up than ever.

First, she'd insisted on remodeling their kitchen. And maybe it had needed enlarging and upgrading. But looking at Cindy's old-fashioned, outdated kitchen and knowing the kinds of meals she whipped out . . . well, it made no sense. After the kitchen, Jane redecorated their whole house, and he began to worry that having an empty nest was going to empty his wallet. He even encouraged her to get a job or work in his office, but she wasn't having it. Then he suggested volunteering at church, but she claimed there was too much to be done at home.

In the last ten years, her obsession over cleanliness and order and perfection had increased to an almost intolerable level. Okay, it was downright intolerable! If he didn't escape from his home through work and playing golf on Saturdays and poker on Thursdays, he knew he'd be miserable. Sometimes, although he'd never admitted this to anyone, he was worried she was spinning into something like OCD. He'd read up on it and even mentioned it to her once, but she'd just laughed and made excuses. And, to be fair, he hadn't noticed any obsessive habits that crossed over into compulsions. She didn't turn lights off and on or check locks or insist they go back home to ensure the coffee maker wasn't still on—although it turned off automatically anyway. But sometimes he wondered if those behaviors were just around the corner.

"Hey, Rob," Erik said as he joined him in the kitchen, getting a beer from the fridge. "Halftime's over, better get back in there." He held up his IPA. "Need a brewski to go with that?" He nodded to Rob's plate. "Mandy made that. Her mom's recipe. Don't tell her, but Cindy's is still better."

"Well, this was pretty good." Rob reached for a second beer, his wife's warning voice in his ear, but he didn't care.

"Jonathon is still taking bets on the game. The 49ers might be down, but I'm predicting a comeback."

"Rob!" Cindy said as she came into the kitchen. "I never got a chance to say hello and thank you for coming. I heard Jane isn't feeling well. I hope she's not getting what we had."

"It's just a headache. By the way, happy birthday."

"Jocelyn just showed me the gift you brought." She beamed at him. "You didn't have to do that, but I'm glad you did. Presents are fun. And I love the mug. The caption on it is perfect. Thanks so much. And tell Jane thanks, too, and that I hope she gets better soon."

"I will." Rob made an uneasy nod, hating to feel deceptive.

"I have some homemade chicken broth in my freezer. Maybe I'll bring her some tomorrow if she's still under the weather."

"Thanks." Rob forced a smile.

"Now, come on." Erik tugged his arm. "Sounds like they're playing."

Rob's smile turned genuine. "Excuse me, birthday girl, but it seems the 49ers are calling."

* * *

The game was over, much to the dismay of the 49ers and their fans. Rob lost his ten-dollar bet, and Erik invited him out to the garage to see his latest woodworking project. The McEntires' garage, like the rest of their home, was a colorful scene of muddled mess, but somehow Erik picked his way through the minefield to a workbench. Amid a bunch of random tools and things stood a row of birdhouses in various stages of construction. "I feel kind of silly about these, but my granddaughter Arianna had me make one for her birthday last summer, and suddenly all my grands claimed they needed one too. I hope to get these all done in time for Christmas."

"I'm impressed. You could go into business. Or retirement." He chuckled. "Are you thinking of retiring?"

"Well, I'm sixty-seven now. Cindy keeps urging me to pull the plug and enjoy life more." He looked around the garage and sighed. "But I'm worried that if I retire, I'll end up spending all my time organizing this disaster area, and that sounds like a heckofa lot more work than my job at the insurance office."

Rob laughed. "I see what you mean. I'm not eager to retire either."

"Not for this reason." Erik gestured at the mess. "Your garage is immaculate, Rob. I've seen it. I think you could eat off the floor in there."

Rob actually rolled his eyes. "Tempting at times."

"Huh?"

"You want to know the real reason I don't want to retire?"

"Sure."

Rob let out a long sigh, wondering how much he should say but feeling like he might explode if he didn't get to talk to someone. And Erik seemed like an understanding friend. Besides, he knew Jane. He'd been in their home.

"The truth is, it's a little unsettling to imagine being home all the time, 24/7, you know?"

Erik's brow creased slightly. "You mean being underfoot?"

"Sort of. Jane is so fastidious that it can be, uh, hard to relax."

Erik put the lid on an open paint can. "Oh, yeah. I get that. Truth is, I sorta feel like I have to be in my Sunday best at your house."

"You're not the only one." Rob frowned. "Erik, can I ask you something—and get an honest answer?"

"Sure, anytime." He pushed the can away.

"Do you know what OCD is?"

"Obsessive-compulsive disorder? Sure, I watch old reruns of *Monk*."

Rob's smile felt weak. "Yeah, like that. Do you think Jane's got it?"

With a thoughtful look, Erik shrugged. "I suppose it's possible. Kinda makes sense. Have you ever mentioned it to her?"

Rob's laugh sounded hollow to his own ears. "Are you kidding? I even made her watch a few *Monk* episodes with me a couple years ago. And I asked her about why he was like that, and she said he was just eccentric and charming. She couldn't see the dysfunction."

"Sometimes they're the last to know."

"I guess. But the thing is, she's getting worse, and it's hard to live with her." He looked pointedly at Erik. "Probably hard to be her neighbor too."

Erik just laughed. "I have a feeling it's harder on her than us." He shrugged. "We're so busy with our lives and kids and stuff, we don't pay her much mind."

"And Cindy is always trying to befriend her."

"Well, we go to the same church, Rob. And we are supposed to love our neighbors. Even if they're, well, difficult."

"Hello, there in the garage?" called a male voice.

"Well, I'll be, that sounds like one of my boys." Erik tried to see the door, but it was blocked by a pile of boxes. "Malcolm, is that you?"

"You guessed it!" The young man picked his way toward them. "Mr. Bradshaw!" Malcolm looked surprised. "I didn't expect to find you here." They shook hands.

"Your dad was just showing me his Christmas projects."

"Wow, Dad, when you said you were working on a bird-house, I didn't realize you were going into production. These are awesome."

"All the grands seemed to think they needed one. So, what are you doing here?"

"Came for Mom's birthday. Figured better late than never. And Mom didn't seem to mind." He turned back to Rob. "By the way, I brought a surprise for you."

"Huh?" Rob blinked.

"Your daughter came with me."

"Olivia?" Rob was stunned. "She's here?"

"In the house with Mom and the ladies. Last I saw they were shoving food at her, but I wanted to say hey to Dad."

Erik grabbed his son into a big bear hug. "Well, I'm so glad to see you, son. Thanks for coming. But you might have to sleep on the floor." He started to rattle off how many kids and grandkids were camped out in the various rooms."

"We have an empty guest room," Rob said suddenly, despite knowing he probably shouldn't. "Why not stay with us, Malcolm?"

"Seriously?" Malcolm looked surprised.

"Absolutely. The guest room is always ready but rarely gets used."

"We're only here for one night," Malcolm told him.

"And you came together?" Rob studied the tall young man. "How did that happen?"

"Well, sir, I might as well let the cat out of the bag."

"Sounds like veterinarian talk to me," Erik teased. "Did you hear he's practicing at a vet clinic in Salem?"

"That's right. Congratulations on graduating vet school, Malcolm. Or should I call you *Dr.* McEntire?"

Malcolm laughed. "First name's good."

"So, tell me, what proverbial cat are you talking about?" Rob asked.

"Well, Olivia and I met by chance at the clinic where I work." He quickly explained about her work friend's feline trouble while Rob impatiently waited.

"And?"

"Well, we sort of hit it off. I mean we've always been friends. But this, well, it's different." His cheeks actually reddened a bit. "More serious."

Rob didn't know what to say and felt his brows arching as he imagined Jane's reaction to this news. "Well, Malcolm . . . Olivia is a fine girl. Not that I'm biased." He forced a nervous chuckle. "And I'm happy you two ran into each other like that."

Erik slapped his son's back. "We've always loved Olivia. She was over here so much she felt like one of the family."

"That's what she says too, Dad."

"So, are you two planning to make this a permanent arrangement?" Erik asked eagerly. "Setting a date?"

"Dad." Malcolm shook his head. "Don't rush things. We're

only dating right now. I mean, it's exclusive and all. But we're not in any big hurry."

"Well, your mom will be thrilled." Erik beamed. "Does she know?"

"Not exactly. But I saw a glint in her eye when she hugged Olivia and figured I should give you a heads-up." Malcolm turned to Rob. "So, is that invitation to stay at your house still good? Or would you prefer to think it over and, uh, maybe consult your wife?"

Rob thought for a good long moment, then slowly shook his head. "No need to consult the missus. I invited you, Malcolm. It's my home and you are welcome." He chuckled. "Might be just the right medicine for Jane to have an unexpected guest."

But he was thinking of an old saying his grandmother quipped when dosing him with some family remedy—"kill or cure." For all he knew, that might be true in Jane's case. Because if Olivia and Malcolm were truly getting serious, Jane would probably faint or throw a fit. Rob knew how to dial 911 and administer CPR, but hopefully it wouldn't come down to that.

five

THE PARTY was winding down some when Olivia's dad suggested she head home before him to surprise her mom, adding, "And you can let her know to expect a houseguest."

She already knew that Dad had invited Malcolm to stay overnight at their house. Although she was pleasantly surprised by her father's hospitality, she wasn't sure it was a good idea. But how could she cancel this plan without looking inhospitable to Malcolm? Although it seemed unfair of Dad to make her spring it on Mom, she agreed. Bracing herself, she thanked her host and made the short trek home, silently praying with each step. Maybe Mom would be okay with it. After all, she prided herself on being the perfect hostess . . . well, when it was a guest she'd invited. Never with those messy McEntires, as her mom liked to call them.

"Olivia!" Jane exclaimed as Olivia came quietly into the house. "What on earth are you doing here?" She peered out the front window. "I didn't see your car. But you probably had to park on the next block thanks to those neighbors."

She scowled out the window. "That red SUV has its wheels in my planting strip."

Olivia glanced outside. "But it's only on the bark, not hurting the bushes."

"Yes, but if it were summer, I'd have annuals growing there." Jane's tone was sharper than usual. "I'm hoping and praying they'll sell their place before next summer. That house is too big for just two people, and they're both in their sixties now. It'll be hard to keep it up. Not that they ever did." Her brow creased as she turned back to Olivia, then broke into a smile. "I'm sorry, honey. Listen to me going on like that." She gave her daughter a stiff hug. "It's wonderful to see you. I have some dinner I can warm up. I made it for your dad, but he's been next door all day, so I finally put it in the fridge."

"I already ate, but thanks." Olivia didn't mention it was the McEntires' house she'd eaten at. No sense poking a hornet's nest.

"Well, what are you doing here? Is something wrong?" Jane's head tilted to one side. "Did you lose your job?"

"No, nothing like that." Olivia glanced toward the kitchen. "I could use a cup of tea."

"Of course." Jane linked her arm in Olivia's. "I just got a new herbal tea I haven't even tried."

As her mom fussed about the immaculate kitchen, Olivia sat at the breakfast bar, planning her words. Finally, the tea was set down, along with some store-bought chocolate mint cookies.

Olivia sipped her tea. "This is good, Mom. I'll have to get the name before I leave."

"Yes, of course. How long can you stay?"

"We have to go back tomorrow."

"We?" Jane's thin brows arched. "Who's with you?"

"I, uh, got a ride here with Malcolm McEntire."

Jane's eyes grew large. "You mean, Malcolm *next door* McEntire?"

Olivia explained how they'd crossed paths several months ago. "I couldn't believe it when he was the vet treating Shannon's cat."

"Shannon?"

"Just a work friend. Anyway, there was Malcolm, looking so grown-up and handsome in his vet jacket. The next thing I knew, we were meeting for coffee and laughing about old times."

"Old times?"

"Oh, you know. Growing up next door. I spent a lot of time at their house. They were so fun and loud . . . it was kind of like belonging to a big family."

Her mom's scowl returned as she folded and refolded the pretty floral cocktail napkin. "So, you came home with Malcolm McEntire."

"Yes, at the last minute he wanted to make an appearance for his mom's birthday."

She grimly nodded. "And he's over there at Cindy's now? And you'll ride back to the city with him tomorrow?"

"That's right." Olivia bit into a cookie, ignoring the fact it tasted like flavored sawdust in her mouth. She could tell that somehow her mother had suspected something. Perhaps Cindy had given hints. But why this cat and mouse game? What did her mother hope to gain from it?

Jane looked intently at Olivia. "So . . . is this, um, this friendship just that? A friendship? Or is there more going on?"

Olivia washed the cookie bite down with tea then shrugged. "I'm not totally sure, Mom. But I know I like him . . . a lot. And he seems to like me."

"Olivia. Of all the men on the planet, you would have to get involved with a McEntire. Was this intentional? A way to hurt me?"

"Oh, Mom." Olivia took in a calming breath. "The McEntires are wonderful people. I was just in their home, and it was filled with love and laughter and good food. I wish you'd gone over there for Cindy's—"

"Please, you sound like your father now." Jane stood, carrying her teacup and dish to the sink, where she rinsed and re-rinsed the china.

"Speaking of Dad . . ." Olivia decided to just bite the bullet. "He invited Malcolm to stay in our guest room tonight. He wanted me to tell you."

Jane spun around with a dropped jaw. "What—"

"Speak of the devil," Olivia interrupted. "That sounds like them now." She eagerly stood and went out to greet them, giving her father a warning glance. "I just told Mom to expect a guest." She smiled at Malcolm, noticing a bundle under his arm. "I see you brought some overnight things. How about I show you the guest room." Tugging his elbow, she led him upstairs, trying to ignore the sound of her parents' voices downstairs. Not that they were loud, but she could hear the sharpness in Mom's tone and the defensiveness in Dad's. Thankfully, Malcolm looked oblivious. Or maybe he was just being polite.

"I've never been up here before." Malcolm looked around the immaculate guest room, recently redecorated in shades of creamy white and pale green. "Pretty room." He set his bundle on a chair.

"Uh-huh." She nervously pretended to level a pastel floral painting that was already perfectly straight.

"Are you okay?" he asked. "You seem uneasy."

"Well, you know." She turned to face him. "My mom . . . she can be . . ."

"A little difficult." His smile looked slightly stiff. "Believe me, I *know*, Olivia. Maybe it's not a good idea for me to be here. I don't mind sleeping on the floor at my house."

She felt a surge of fresh resolve. "No, my dad is absolutely right. This is his house, too, and he invited you. And it's my home." She smoothed a hand over the creamy white down comforter, knowing her mother always chose the very best. "And I know for a fact this is a very comfortable bed. My mother would never settle for anything less." Even in her guest room. Not that she practiced much hospitality. Her mom's obsession over perfection had always scared off visitors. Olivia bit her lip in frustration, imagining all that could go wrong with Malcolm's overnight visit, and how her mother could scare him off too.

"Don't worry," he assured her, as if reading her thoughts. "I'll be on my best behavior." He pursed his lips. "Although I gotta admit, all these light-colored furnishings and linens do make me a little nervous. I promise not to put my dirty feet on anything." He chuckled, but she suspected he wasn't kidding, and as they went downstairs, where her parents were now actually arguing, Malcolm excused himself to go back to his house.

"I promised my siblings that I'd play some new trivia game with them. I used to win at Trivial Pursuit, and apparently my sister Jocelyn wants to challenge me." He looked at Olivia. "You're welcome to join us if you'd like."

Olivia glanced at her mother and, seeing a frown of disapproval, she thanked him and declined, promising to leave the door unlocked for him. But when Malcolm left, she wished she was with him. She would've preferred sleeping on a floor over there over the most comfortable bed in her parents' home.

* * *

After a restless night's sleep, Olivia got up early and dressed. But before leaving her old bedroom, she neatly put everything back into place. No point in rocking Mom's boat any more than necessary. As she made her bed, she tried not to replay last night's conversation—make that *inquisition*—with her mom. Dad had wisely retired early, but he'd still been clearly upset by his wife's unreasonable behavior. Olivia had been too. But she'd tried to reason with her mom, even suggesting she might need professional help. But that just made everything worse, until Olivia had to excuse herself to bed too. She didn't hear Malcolm sneaking quietly into the house until close to midnight, but after he got safely to his room, she went down to check the door and turn out the lights. Didn't want to leave anything for Mom to complain about the next day.

The house still seemed quiet as she crept down the stairs, but unless it was hopeful imagining, she smelled coffee coming from the kitchen. And since her mom avoided caffeine, Olivia suspected her dad was up early.

"Good morning," she said quietly from behind him, making him jump.

"Oh, it's you." He smiled. "Thought it was your mom."

"I kept her up pretty late last night," she confessed. "Hopefully she's sleeping in."

"Hopefully." His smile faded. "Unfortunately, but not surprisingly, she didn't sleep too well last night. Tossed and turned into the wee hours."

"I'm sorry, Dad. Maybe I shouldn't have—"

"This is not your fault, Olivia." He looked intently into her eyes. "Your mother's . . . preferences have gotten more and more extreme, and I'm the one who invited Malcolm."

"I know. But just the fact that I'm dating Malcolm is so hard on her. It's almost as if she thinks I purposely did this to upset her."

He nodded. "Uh-huh. Seems par for the course." He reached for the coffee pot. "Want some high-octane joe?"

"Absolutely." She went to fridge to look for cream and settled for 2 percent milk. "Mom must still be on her no-fat kick. Doesn't she know that some fats are good for us?"

"You're welcome to tell her. But maybe you want to pick your battles." He handed her a steaming mug and then led her to his den, closing the door behind them.

She sunk into one of his oversized sofas—in her opinion, the only comfortable seating in their home. "Oh, Dad, what am I going to do if this gets even more serious with Malcolm and me?"

"And you're hoping it will?"

She simply nodded, then sipped her coffee, watching his expression change from concern to what almost looked like hopefulness.

"Well," he said slowly, "you and Malcolm in a serious relationship . . . it might be just what your mother needs."

"How's that?"

"Might help her to see how unreasonable and dysfunctional her perfectionist ways have become. Not to mention impossible to live with."

She felt a wave of compassion. "Oh, Dad," she exclaimed. "I don't know how you do it. Year after year. At least I got to escape."

"Sometimes I wonder." He set his mug down with a *clunk* right on the wooden coffee table, ignoring the coasters stacked neatly there. "I've considered leaving, Olivia. I hate to admit it, but I have moments when I wonder how much a grown man can take. I even imagine that my leaving could be a wake-up call for your mother. Then I remember our wedding vows, my commitment to the Lord . . . and I feel guilty."

"I kind of have similar feelings. I mean, it's not like I can divorce my own mother, but I do imagine moving so far away that I never have to interact with her."

"Oh, honey, I would miss you."

She smiled sadly. "I would miss you too."

"Well, I'm really glad you and Malcolm came this weekend. It's got me thinking about a harebrained idea I got while watching some weird TV movie."

"What's that?"

"An intervention."

"Seriously? What would you do? Get a professional here?"

"Maybe if necessary. But I thought of family and friends to start with. Not that Jane has many friends. I mean, there are a couple of sweet church gals that put up with her. And whether she can admit it or not, she's got good friends in Cindy and Erik. Despite our Hatfield and McCoy history, they are habitually kind and gracious to her. It sometimes makes me feel even more guilty."

"They're good people."

He just nodded. "Anyway, I've imagined this intervention where your grandmother comes for an extended visit. Maybe even during the holidays."

Olivia felt her eyes getting big. "No way, Dad. That could be seriously messed up."

"Exactly. I'd like to mess up your mom's world. And who better than Lulu to do that?"

She considered this. "You make a good point."

"And maybe, with this new development with Malcolm, maybe we could use that as an excuse to involve his family."

"New development?" She wondered just how much Dad knew. She hadn't told him, or anyone, her true feelings. Dad just smiled his knowing smile, which was both reassuring and aggravating.

"To be honest, this *new* development with Malcolm might end before it gets fully started."

Dad looked clearly disappointed. "Why?"

"I'm afraid Mom and her relationship with his family could put the kibosh on the whole thing. Talk about a romance killer."

Dad rubbed his chin and picked up his coffee mug, slowly sipping before looking at her. "Do you really like him, Olivia? I mean, do you think he might be the one?"

She didn't know what to say. "I really do like him. And I guess I hope he's the one. He's quite a guy, Dad."

"I know. I like him too."

She smiled, relieved that at least one of her parents approved, but then she heard something in the kitchen. "Sounds like Mom is up."

Dad closed his eyes and let out a long sigh. "I guess we should brace ourselves for whatever lies ahead."

"It's Sunday. Don't you guys usually go to church?"

"Usually. But seeing that we have a guest . . . I don't know."

They both turned to see the den door open.

"Oh, you're in here," Jane said. "Good morning."

They greeted her and listened to her tell them what she

planned to fix for breakfast, but when Olivia offered to help, Jane immediately and expectedly declined.

"Well, just holler if you change your mind," Olivia called out as Jane firmly closed the door. "She still seems mad," she whispered to her dad.

He just nodded.

"Back to your intervention idea," she said quietly. "Are you serious?"

"Serious as a heart attack."

She grimaced. Hopefully it wouldn't come down to that.

"So, if you and Malcolm are still together in a couple weeks, and your mom told me you promised to come home for a few days during the holidays, and I assume Malcolm will be at his folks' place . . . do you think you two would like to be involved in this intervention?"

She tried to imagine what that would look like and realized she couldn't even wrap her head around it. But the idea of confronting her mom with a group for an intervention made her feel slightly sick inside. Well, unless it worked.

"I guess so, Dad. But there are so many ways it could go wrong. It'd be disingenuous to act like I'm not worried."

"You and me both. But sometimes drastic situations call for drastic measures."

"I guess." She sipped her now lukewarm but still very strong coffee laced with its pathetic excuse for creamer. "Do you think Grandma Lulu would even come?"

"I don't know, but I'm willing to find out."

She slowly shook her head as realization of the disaster ahead suddenly manifested in her imagination. "Wow, Dad, this could be a very messy Christmas."

He held up his coffee mug in a toast. “Okay, partner, let’s drink to that. To a very messy Christmas.”

She stretched over to clink her mug against his. Hopefully they would all survive with health and sanity intact, but Olivia had some very serious doubts.

six

FEELING GUILTY for his plan to sneak out of the Bradshaw house without speaking to anyone, Malcolm made a quick note of apology to his hosts, leaving it on his neatly made bed. Okay, *neatly* was a stretch. He knew it wasn't up to Mrs. Bradshaw's high standards, but at least he'd tried. He hated to admit it, but being in that house felt downright creepy. And *creepy* wasn't a word he'd used since grade school.

At first he'd thought it might be a nice departure to stay in such a picture-perfect home. Sort of like a high-end Airbnb. But it didn't take long to feel uncomfortable. It wasn't just the over-the-top neatness—the whole house felt stifling. And after rehanging the towel he'd used so it could dry, although he suspected it should go in a laundry hamper somewhere, he got the unexplainable urge to let out a loud howl. Sort of how one might feel amid a silent crowd at a funeral that runs too long.

By the time he was sneaking back to his parents' house, he felt like a prisoner of war upon release, and when he walked through the front door, seeing siblings, nieces, and nephews in various stages of rumpled dress and scruffy hair, he knew he'd been delivered.

"Free at last, free at last," he proclaimed, "thank God Almighty, I'm free at last."

His dad laughed as he emerged from the dining room with an oversized mug of coffee. "That bad?"

Malcolm blew out a sigh. "It's a different world over there."

"Well, the gals have set out a scrumptious spread in here." Erik led the way to the cluttered dining room, where the table was crowded with various dishes of breakfast foods.

Malcolm grinned and picked up a plate from the mismatched stack at one end. "Home sweet home," he said quietly.

"So, how did it go over there?" Erik asked as he cut into some kind of baked egg concoction that looked yummy.

"Honestly?" Malcolm picked up a blueberry muffin and sniffed with appreciation.

"Yeah."

Malcolm glanced around to see he and Dad were the only ones in earshot, then lowered his voice. "It was creepy."

Erik's brows arched. "Creepy?"

"That's not the right word. But it just felt so weird. I couldn't wait to get out of there. Kind of like visiting a foreign country—a hostile one. Or maybe another planet."

Erik chuckled. "Yeah, I sometimes feel a little like that when I'm over there."

"Do you go over there much?"

"Not much. I don't feel particularly welcome, if you know what I mean."

"I didn't feel particularly welcome either. Mrs. Bradshaw was not happy to see me. And she wasn't very good at hiding it."

Erik's brow creased. "Does this affect how you feel about Olivia?"

"I don't know, Dad. To be honest, it scares me a little. I remember hearing once that before you marry a girl, you should take a good hard look at her mother because that's what you could end up with."

"Marry?" Erik laid two strips of bacon on his already full plate.

"Yeah, that's premature, I know. But even if you're just dating someone, I think it could apply. And it doesn't help that Mrs. Bradshaw can't stand our family. I mean, seriously, Dad, what would that be like?"

Erik glumly shook his head. "Those are valid points."

"Malcolm!" exclaimed his mother, coming through the door with a plate of sausages in her hands. "You're here for breakfast. How nice. I thought you'd probably eat at the Bradshaws' house."

"When all these great cooks are over here?" he said in a jovial tone.

She set the dish down. "Well, there's enough food here to feed an army. Are you going to church with us this morning? That's why we're getting such an early start. The whole family has promised to go to first service with us in honor of my birthday. Isn't that sweet? How about you?"

He nodded, munching on a crispy strip of bacon. "Sure, I'd like to go too."

His mom stepped closer with a conspiratorial glint in her eye. "How did it go over at Olivia's house?"

He shrugged and exchanged glances with Dad. "Oh, it was pretty quiet. And the bed was super comfy." To his relief, two of his brothers entered the room, arguing about politics like they often did at family gatherings.

"How about if we ban political debates," Erik told his sons, "in honor of Mom's birthday weekend."

They reluctantly toned it down, and Malcolm carried his plate into the kitchen to express gratitude to the creators of the breakfast feast. Like always, the chatter was fast and witty and familiar, and before long, they were all laughing together.

When it was time to leave for church, Malcolm told his dad he wanted to take his own car and get gas. As he went out, he glanced over at the Bradshaws' house and considered asking Olivia to join him, but for some reason he just couldn't ring that doorbell. He thought about texting her but convinced himself she might be sleeping in and didn't want to bother her. Maybe he'd see her at church.

The McEntire family filled almost two full rows in the sanctuary. As they all sat together, singing familiar songs and listening to a sermon about Advent, Malcolm thought about Olivia. If, and it was a huge if, they ever decided to get married, the ceremony would most likely take place right here, with his family and their friends filling much of the church on the groom's side. He wondered who would be on the bride's side. The Bradshaws had never seemed to have many friends. Not like his family anyway. And why was he even thinking about it? Thoughts of the ice-cold Mrs. Bradshaw filled him with apprehension. What if Olivia did turn out to be like that? After all, they say the apple doesn't fall far from the tree. But then he looked at his siblings and realized how all of them were completely different from each other . . . and for a moment he felt hopeful.

When the service ended and he was leaving, he noticed old Doc Wheeler in the back and decided to exchange a greeting.

"Do you remember me?" he asked.

"Of course, I do. Malcolm McEntire." Dr. Wheeler shook his hand. "I hear you got your degree in veterinary medicine a year or so ago."

"It's actually been almost six years." Malcolm explained about the vet clinic he worked at.

"Do you like that? Being a vet in the city?"

"Well, the experience is good. But we're an emergency clinic, open 24/7, so my hours are pretty random."

Dr. Wheeler nodded. "I get a few late-night calls too—emergencies. It used to be easier back when I was younger. Marsha keeps telling me it's time to think about retiring." His eyes grew thoughtful. "Or hire a younger vet to help out."

Malcolm stood straighter, smiling with confidence. "Well, if you ever get serious about that, I hope you'll keep me in mind."

"Really?" Dr. Wheeler gave him a good hard look. "You know I treat livestock as well as family pets."

"I know." Malcolm nodded eagerly. "I've missed that since interning."

Dr. Wheeler rubbed his chin. "Are you doing anything now? Want to meet for a cup of coffee and kick this around some more? Marsha stays on to help with Sunday school in second service so I'm at loose ends. Well, unless I get a call."

Malcolm agreed to meet him at a nearby coffee shop, and as soon as they sat down with their drinks, they were discussing the latest advances in veterinary medicine, the way Dr. Wheeler's practice had grown in the past several years, and even the possibility of a job. When they wrapped it up, it was nearly noon, and Dr. Wheeler explained it was time to pick up his wife. They exchanged phone numbers and shook hands.

"Do you plan on being around for the holidays?" Dr. Wheeler asked as they were heading outside.

"Yeah. I'm taking off a week at Christmas. Our vets take turns on holidays and vacation time, but it wasn't really my turn yet, so I'll be putting in a lot of overtime between now and then to work out a switch."

"Okay, let's talk again when you're back in town." Dr. Wheeler patted him on the back. "Tell your folks hello for me."

As Malcolm got gas, he replayed their conversation. He hadn't been promised anything, but he still felt pretty hopeful. He realized it could involve more work and more hours than his current job, but in the long run, it would be worth it. In time the old vet would retire, and he'd need someone to take over the clinic. It would be a dream come true.

He was just leaving the gas station when his phone pinged with a text. Olivia. She was worried he'd left for Salem without her. At the stoplight, he reassured her he was still in town and would soon be at her place, suggesting she be ready to go.

He didn't ask her to be waiting on the front porch but knew he didn't want to go up to that door and go back inside that house. To his relief, she was outside waiting when he arrived.

"I really thought you'd left without me," she said as she got in the car.

He explained about slipping out early to spend more time with his family. "Didn't you get my note?"

"Yeah, but that was hours ago. And your car was gone."

"I wouldn't have stranded you like that," he said in a slightly defensive tone. "Sorry to worry you."

"It's okay. No big deal. Gave me more time with my parents."

"Did you go to church?" he asked. "I didn't see you at first service."

"Dad went to second service, but Mom was set on decorating for Christmas. She always decorates on the same day—and this was the day. Like her countdown to Christmas. I decided to stick around."

"Uh-huh." He wanted to sound interested but really didn't care to hear about it. "So, you helped her decorate?"

"Yeah . . . I guess . . . sort of . . ." Olivia's tone faltered, and she turned to look out the side window. She seemed disconnected, which was fine with him. He wasn't ready to talk about anything that mattered, and he'd never liked chitchat. Part of him wanted to tell her about his serendipitous meeting with Dr. Wheeler, but another part of him felt cautious. Because, really, he didn't know where this relationship was going, and suddenly the two-hour drive felt like it would be very long—long and quiet.

seven

OLIVIA DIDN'T WANT to talk—to anyone. Including Malcolm as he drove them home. At first she thought it was because he had abandoned her—or that was how it had felt. But it wasn't long until she realized it was her mother getting under her skin. She would have preferred to have been irritated with Malcolm since she knew that would pass quickly. But she knew it was her mother. As usual.

She hadn't really wanted to help Mom with the Christmas decorating. She knew better. She'd helped Dad get the artificial tree set up in front of the living room window, keeping her negative opinions about fake trees to herself. She knew that would only create an unwanted battle, pitting her and Dad against Mom. But after testing the lights, Dad announced he was heading out to church and invited Olivia to join him. She was about to say yes, but seeing Mom's forlorn expression filled her with daughterly guilt. After all, it wasn't like she visited the home front very often. And it had been ages since she'd helped Mom decorate for Christmas. Why not while away an hour, hopefully less, with her mother while waiting for Malcolm to return? Especially since he'd said he wanted an early start on the road this morning.

She sighed and slumped back in the car seat, crossing her arms and closing her eyes, prepared to feign napping. The truth was she wasn't ready to engage with Malcolm quite yet. Not that she exactly blamed him for her miserable morning, but she wanted to escape brooding over him . . . and she began to replay the morning with Mom.

It had all started out innocently enough. Olivia had offered to help carry the neatly stacked storage bins from the garage. Each plastic bin was clearly labeled, thanks to the label maker her mom credited Martha Stewart's ingenuity for. And when they began to open the carefully packed bins, every item was predictably wrapped in pale blue tissue paper.

"You always pack everything so carefully," Olivia absently said as she unwound a crystal snowflake hanging by a ribbon. She twirled the piece in the sunlight coming in from the front window. "Pretty."

"Pretty fragile. Do be careful with that," Mom warned. "That's my Swarovski box."

"Wow, really?"

"Each piece in there retails for about a hundred dollars. Although they were less when I got them, plus I got a quantity discount."

Olivia stared at the box, guessing the total contents' replacement value could be around two grand. "My goodness. Maybe you should handle this box."

"Yes. How about you get on the stepladder and I'll unwrap and hand them to you, and you can place them where I point."

"Okay." Olivia wanted to jokingly ask Mom if she had a remote control, and Olivia could be the robot, but knew better.

While Olivia perched on the ladder, her mom used a yardstick from her craft room as a pointer, specifically instructing where and how to hang the precious snowflakes. By the time they got to the lower branches, Olivia felt so nervous, she wished she'd put on an extra layer of antiperspirant after her shower that morning.

"Maybe you should take it from here," she suggested. "I can work on something else." Hopefully something less breakable and less expensive. To her relief, her mom agreed.

"How about this bin?" Olivia read the label to herself: *Lladró*. She wasn't sure what that meant, but the wrapped pieces looked large and didn't seem too risky. And, unwrapping the first large piece, it turned out to be one of Mom's porcelain angels. Fragile, yes, but not as delicate as the crystal snowflakes. She carried the first angel over to the cleared and dusted walnut table in the foyer. It was long and narrow with a gilt frame mirror above it. Normally it held a crystal vase with flowers, but it was where her mother always placed her collection of angel statues, which Olivia had never paid much attention to, except that they were too formal for her taste.

Olivia gently set the figurine down with satisfaction. So far so good. She returned to the living room, pausing to look at the tree and out the front window, hoping to see Malcolm's blue SUV outside, but no luck. So she unwrapped another angel.

"It's been years since I helped you decorate for Christmas," she commented after setting the second angel on the sideboard. "But if I remember, you didn't have all these fancy things back when I was young."

"You've been away from home for so long. First college, then your career." Her mom's voice was wistful. "I've done the decorating by myself for years."

"I didn't even help you do this before college," Olivia commented. "In fact, the last time I remember helping, I was about eleven or twelve." She didn't mention how she used to get scolded for carelessness, or how they'd gotten into a hot argument one year over how to hang the silver tinsel. Olivia had wanted to do it in clumps that year, hoping to finish the task quickly, but her mom had insisted on doing it one at a time, strand by strand. It had seemed a silly waste of time to Olivia, and that was the end of it. Not many Christmases later, Mom's decor was ramped up to create a more "elegant" Christmas, and Olivia had lost all interest. As a teenager, she hadn't minded being left out, and their home turned into a holiday "show place," or show-off place, as Olivia had called it to her friends.

"Whatever happened to the old nativity set you used to let me put up on the table? The one Grandma Lulu gave me when I was little."

"Oh, that old thing? I think I donated it to a church rummage sale."

"You gave it away?" Olivia put her hands on her hips, glaring at her mother. "But it was mine."

"Oh, I didn't think you'd mind. It was a pretty cheesy set. Plastic and paint chipping off the pieces. And the stable had fallen apart."

"But I loved it, Mom. I would've saved it for my children . . . well, if that ever happens. But, really, it was mine. You shouldn't have gotten rid of it."

Her mother looked up from hanging a low snowflake with an exasperated expression. "Well, look at all these fabulous pieces you will get someday, Olivia. The Swarovski and Lladró and lots of other costly treasures. Surely you and your someday children should appreciate that."

"I loved that old nativity set," she muttered, more to herself than her mother, turning away to unwrap another angel. How many were there anyway?

"What?" Mom's sharp tone insinuated she'd heard her.

"It's just that, as a child, the nativity set represented the true meaning of Christmas." Olivia kept her voice even, although her temper was rising. "I always loved setting up the angels and shepherds and little lambs. And the fancy wise men with their gifts that looked sparkly to a four-year-old, and finally I'd stand Joseph and Mary in the stable and baby Jesus in his manger, with some real grass from our yard spread around for hay. And maybe it was only cheap plastic and chipped and wobbly, but to me it felt more real than *this*." She held up the large angel she'd just unwrapped like it was court evidence.

"Be careful with that," Mom warned. "Some of that Lladró is irreplaceable."

Olivia wanted to turn up her nose and shout that she preferred cheesy dime store ornaments to these sparkly, showy things any day, but knew that would only create a real row and make her wait for Malcolm seem even longer. Where was he, anyway? And so she said nothing as she carried the angel to the foyer.

And then it had happened. In her haste and frustration, she'd caught the heel of her boot on the Persian carpet, lost her balance, and, in an attempt to catch herself on the arm of a chair, the figurine had slipped from her hands, crashing into a hundred shiny white shards on the hardwood floor.

Olivia grimaced to remember the awful scene still imprinted in her brain. Why was she even replaying it now? Still slumped down in the passenger seat, she glanced at Malcolm. He seemed totally oblivious to her and her foul mood, or just focused on the road. Or maybe deep in thought. What *was* he thinking about? Probably what a mistake it was to get involved with her and her family. She knew it hadn't been a coincidence that he'd gotten up so early and quietly snuck out. And she knew that was what he'd done because she'd been up early too.

She'd woken before seven with the idea of offering to take him to breakfast in town as a thank-you for giving her a ride yesterday. And hopefully it'd give her a chance to apologize for her cold, sterile home, her mom's bad behavior, and the argument he might've overheard between her parents last night. She'd imagined them both laughing over the whole thing. Really, on some level it had been rather humorous. At least it had seemed that way earlier. Now she wasn't sure Malcolm would even see the humor in it. She didn't think she could.

If she felt like talking with Malcolm right now, she might confess about breaking her mother's most valued piece of Lladró. A rare piece, according to Mom, worth around a thousand dollars! Olivia still felt sick to think she'd dropped it like that, almost like a Freudian mistake. But she felt even more sickened at how her mother had reacted. As if Olivia had done it purposely! Even Olivia's tears and sincere apology had seemed to fall on deaf ears. And so she'd acted like a child and run to her room, watching out the window for Malcolm's SUV to turn down their street before sneaking down the stairs and out the front door to skulk away before things got worse.

She snuck another peek at Malcolm. Focused on the winding road, he didn't even know she was looking. Perhaps he'd forgotten she was even here. She studied his profile, admiring the straight nose and strong jaw, and her heart softened. Malcolm was a good man. Probably too good to put up with her and her difficult family.

For a split second she was tempted to spill her guts and tell him about her heartache with Mom, as well as her dad's idea about an intervention for Mom, and about bringing in her free-spirited grandmother to really shake things up. As if that would be the magic bullet. But she knew an intervention was a long shot at best. And she suspected Malcolm wouldn't care anyway. It looked like he had his mind on other, more important things . . . and who could blame him?

eight

BEFORE CALLING LULU with an invitation to spend the holidays with them, Rob did a bit of research on performing an intervention. Then he called Justin Larsson from their church and arranged to meet him at the coffeehouse on Thursday. Justin was one of a team of three pastors who also did family counseling—and someone who Jane seemed to respect. Probably because the attractive younger pastor was always neatly dressed, in a buttoned-up sort of way.

"Thanks for meeting me." Rob shook Justin's hand and nodded to a chair. "I see you got your coffee."

"How are you doing?" Justin asked as he sat.

"Well, to be honest, I'm feeling a little conflicted."

"How so?"

"This has to do with my wife, Jane." Rob suddenly felt like a betrayer. Maybe he was making a mountain out of a molehill. After all, most people—ones who didn't know Jane well—seemed to assume she was not only perfectly normal but more together than most. An image his wife strove to preserve.

"What sort of problem?" Justin asked. "And don't worry,

I do a lot of couples counseling, and everything you say will stay between us."

"That's not exactly it," Rob confessed. "But I'll admit what I'm about to explain has taken a toll on our marriage." And then Rob opened up about the changes he'd been seeing in Jane, feeling like he was literally spilling his guts. "I really love her, but she is a royal pain. She's ruining relationships all around her." He felt his eyes misting up and used a napkin to blow his nose. "Including our own."

"You mentioned OCD," Justin said carefully. "I assume she's never been diagnosed?"

"Are you kidding? She thinks she's perfectly normal. It's the rest of the world that's a great big mess."

Justin nodded. "So, I'm curious . . . what do you want your next steps to be? I can understand how you needed to get that off your chest and talk to someone, and I'm totally fine with just that. But is there more I can do to help? Should I try to talk to her?"

Rob explained the intervention idea. "Do you think that sounds nuts?"

Justin chuckled. "I don't know. I mean, intervention from loving family and friends often helps addicts to choose to get help. I suppose it couldn't really hurt. Especially if things are as bad as you say. And if Jane can see and admit she has a serious problem, she might be willing to get help."

Rob told him about the idea to invite his mother-in-law for Christmas and to help with the intervention. "Most guys don't get along with their wife's mother, but Lulu is great. I mean, she's a little wacky, but she's lighthearted and fun, kind of an old hippie, and the polar opposite of Jane."

"Might be just the ticket. Anyone else?"

"Our neighbors, the McEntires."

"Good people." Justin nodded.

"We've known them forever, but Jane can't stand them." He explained a bit about the Hatfields and McCoys and that Olivia was now dating Malcolm. "Which is probably why this intervention suddenly feels imperative." Rob made an uneasy smile. "I'd like it if you could come too. Jane respects you, and your perspective would be helpful. Plus, if she's willing to talk about her problem, you seem a good resource."

"I can tell you've given this a lot of thought, Rob. And I'd be honored to help."

They talked a bit more, nailing down possible dates and times, and Justin suggested it might be better to tackle this sooner than later. "To give Jane time to process this and consider what she's heard. We don't want to pull it off right before Christmas and spoil the holidays for everyone involved."

"I agree completely," Rob said as they both stood. "And I can't tell you how relieved I feel to have a plan. I'm going to call Lulu before I go home."

"And I'm going to be praying this goes as well as possible." Justin shook Rob's hand again. "You're a good man, Rob."

"I'm glad you think so. I'm pretty sure my name will be mud when I tell Jane I've invited her mother for Christmas."

Justin chuckled as he pulled on his coat. "I hear we might get snow by next week. Think having a white Christmas will help? It always puts my wife in a jollier mood."

"I guess it couldn't hurt."

Still, as Rob returned to his office down the street, he didn't think the prospect of a white Christmas would lighten the dark cloud hanging over his house right now. Jane had been in a serious funk since Sunday. Whether it was due to the broken porcelain angel, the news that her daughter was dating Malcolm, or life in general, he wasn't sure. But the vibes at home were not good. His wife had stopped decorating midstream, asking him to return the plastic bins to the garage and spending most of her time cleaning and brooding.

Back at the accounting firm, Rob told his receptionist not to disturb him, and, securely tucked into his private and somewhat messy but comfy office, his home away from home, he called his mother-in-law.

"Robbie?" she squealed happily when she picked up. "Is that really you?"

He confirmed his identity, inquired about her health, and then admitted this call was about Jane. "I might need your help."

"Oh, no, is she ill? She's been on my heart lately—"

"No, her health is good. At least physically."

"What's going on, Robbie? Tell me everything."

And so he did, and by the time he finished explaining about the intervention, she burst out laughing.

"Oh, Robbie, that's just rich."

"So you'll come?"

"Of course, I'll come. I've wanted to pull an intervention on my straitlaced daughter for years now. My heart always goes out to the poor girl—and to all of you. You know she's her own worst enemy. To be honest, it was getting hard on me too. Not just her persnickety ways either—although I admit that seeing how stressed my visits made her has kept me from visiting more often—but seeing my own flesh and blood trapped in her glass castle of perfection. Such a sad little life. I felt bad for you and Olivia too. I suppose you've been trapped with her."

"Well, Olivia has managed to escape. For the most part." He

told her about Olivia moving a couple hours away for work, and about Malcolm.

"Oh my goodness!" Lulu's laugh was hearty. "That must've tied Jane's tail in a knot. She can't stand your neighbors."

"Tell me something I don't know." He sighed. "So you'll really come and help me out of this mess?"

"No," she said crisply. "I want to help you *make* a great big mess. A perfect mess. That's just what Jane needs." And suddenly she was tossing out all kinds of crazy ideas to turn Jane's world upside down with chaos.

"I don't know . . ." Suddenly Rob questioned whether any of this was such a great idea. After all, it was his home too. He wasn't ready for a three-ring circus. But he kept his reservations to himself.

"And the holidays are the perfect time for this," she continued. "So many goings-on already. With all the trappings and trimmings. Why, it's a perfect backdrop for an intervention. It will be wonderful."

"Wonderful . . ." he muttered, feeling he had grabbed a tiger by the tail and might be sorry later.

"I'll tie up some loose ends here and come on over. I think I can be there next week. That'll give us some time before Christmas, and plenty of time to shake up Moonbeam's world."

"Moonbeam?"

"Oh, I must've told you before, Rob. It's what I named her as a baby."

As they said goodbye, Rob vaguely remembered the strange name, and how shortly before their wedding Lulu had used that name—and how Jane had thrown such a horrible fit that Lulu apologized and swore she'd never use it again. After things settled down, worried what he was getting into, Rob had demanded to know what the awful scene had been all about. Jane had lightly apologized, claiming her mother was deranged . . . talk about the writing on the wall. Later on, in a tender moment, Jane had confessed that Lulu was telling the truth after all, but that she'd legally changed her name as soon as she was of age—then swore him to secrecy over it. Not wanting any more fits, he'd tucked it all away in some long-lost memory bank. *Moonbeam.* He smiled to himself. Well, hopefully Moonbeam wouldn't turn into a lunatic over her family's plans to help her.

Next, Rob called his daughter. After telling Olivia of Lulu's plans to join them next week, Olivia said she would do her best to get over there as soon as possible, saying she would bring her work with her if necessary.

"I can't promise I'll be there when Grandma comes, but I'll sure try. Because we both know how Mom feels about being surprised."

"Believe me, I know. And springing Grandma Lulu on her is a doozy."

"You'll need some backup, Dad. I'll start getting my ducks in a row to come."

"Thanks, honey. I really appreciate it."

"And the intervention? Did you schedule that too?"

"I'm working on it." He told her about talking to Pastor Justin.

"That's a great idea. And I know it'll be hard, but you're doing the right thing, Dad."

"I hope you're right. After talking to your gung-ho grandmother, I started to have serious second thoughts. Lulu can be a handful."

"I know. But I think it's the right kind of handful. Grandma

Lulu will be hard to take, but she's probably just the right medicine."

"And Erik told me that he and Cindy will come. And I hope you and Malcolm can be here too. Would you mind asking him about it?"

"I, uh, I guess so. Sure." She sounded uncertain, and that concerned Rob.

"Is everything okay with you two? I know things got a little rough the day you left. Everything smoothed out?"

"Uh, sure, Dad. We're fine. And I'll see if he can come. I know he planned on being home for the week before Christmas."

"I don't want to have too many people at the intervention. But we need enough to get her attention and make a valid point. To be honest, the whole thing is starting to remind me of the Mad Hatter's birthday party."

"The un-birthday party," she corrected. "And maybe it'll all lead to a new sort of birthday. Like a rebirth, or wake-up call. Give Mom a second chance at life. Really, Dad, don't doubt yourself. You're doing the right thing." And they said goodbye.

Rob appreciated the encouragement but suspected his daughter was being overly optimistic—kind of like how a hopeful little girl, faced with a giant pile of horse manure, might pick up a shovel and start to dig, expecting to find a pony buried beneath. But in Olivia's case, there was probably no pony. Just a great big pile of disappointment. Rob leaned back in his chair and closed his eyes, wishing he could conjure up some optimism. But at the moment, all he could envision was Jane checking into a psychiatric hospital. He didn't think she would, really—but that's the image he got when thinking about what was ahead.

Rob took in a deep breath and opened his eyes. But really, he reminded himself, would that be any worse than the way they were living now? At this rate, walking on eggshells, trying to do everything perfectly, barely breathing when his wife was looking . . . he was probably the one who would wind up there!

nine

DETERMINED TO FINISH decorating for Christmas, Jane lined up several classical Christmas CDs in their Bose player. She wanted to regain some sort of Christmas spirit. Not so much for herself but to prove to Rob that she was not in need of a psychiatrist. Oh, he'd never actually said that, but she could feel it when he hinted. Rob seemed to think she had obsessive-compulsive disorder. And really, that was absurd. Why should anyone care if she valued order and organization, appreciated a tidy house, and got impatient with those who didn't? Like Cindy next door?

Well, that was ridiculous. Take one stroll through Cindy's house and, unless you were a complete slob or blind, you'd have to know that something was seriously wrong over there. That place was downright dysfunctional and a health hazard to boot. She didn't know why Rob couldn't grasp that. But fretting over this was doing no good.

She'd gotten out a couple of her Christmas bins and attempted to return to putting out her lovely decorations just like she'd done every year. Although she knew exactly where each precious item went and had been doing it perfectly and efficiently in just one day for the last twenty years or so, for some reason she found it to be extremely difficult this year. And she didn't know why. Usually she thrived on getting everything perfectly into place. Since her early twenties, she'd firmly believed the old adage that there was a place for everything and everything should be in its place. And yet, she suddenly felt like she was walking in quicksand, barely able to lift her legs or move her arms.

Deciding she needed a break, she made a cup of her favorite relaxing herbal tea and even got herself a Pepperidge Farm cookie for comfort. Sitting down on her sofa, she took in a deep breath, listening as the string quartet began to play "God Rest Ye Merry Gentlemen," wanting to just soak it in, waiting for some sense of peace and serenity to come.

As she sipped her tea, she tried to remember when she'd first discovered these soothing forms of Christmas music. So much better than "Jingle Bells" and "Deck the Halls," songs that many people favored in hopes of feeling holiday cheer. Those tunes had never made her feel the least bit cheery. And she wasn't even sure why. Or why other people seemed to like them like they did. Couldn't they hear the difference between that trivial tra-la-la and this wonderful quartet?

To be fair, she hadn't grown up with classical music. Her mother had always preferred that tinny, obnoxious music. Lulu had even gotten her an Alvin and the Chipmunks Christmas album one time, thinking Jane would be thrilled. And maybe she had liked it a little at first. But, good grief, she'd probably been four at the time. Something like that would only grind on her last nerve now. Just like any memories from her childhood grated. She sighed, thankful that era was behind her. Some stones really were better left unturned. No telling what one might find. The noise and chaos and mess of her childhood were not unlike what she found next door. As a teenager it had driven her up the wall and made it easy to leave home for college . . . and never go back.

As "Silent Night" began to play, slow and sweet like it should always be, she felt herself relaxing . . . just a smidgeon. Maybe she would regain the energy to finish decorating. She finished her tea and took another deep breath, then slowly stood up, looking around her. Despite it being by the front living room window, the Christmas tree did not fully block the view of Cindy's front yard.

Jane felt her pulse quicken as she surveyed the life-size inflatable Christmas figures littered across the yard. Never mind that the sound of the pump growling 24/7 to keep them inflated was torturous, or that the bright-colored objects that glowed in the dark were so obnoxious. With the cloudy gray sky, they looked gaudier than ever. Who ever thought having Santa with a surfboard was a good idea? And an inflatable manger scene? Who thought that was a good idea? A new addition to the McEntires' menagerie this year was a Grinch with a snarly expression possessively hugging a bag of toys. Was that meant to be a reflection on her? Did they all think she was a Grinch?

She turned her attention to her tree. At least *it* was decorated. With sparkly crystal snowflakes, pale blue icicles, silver glass balls . . . the only thing missing was the pale blue moiré satin ribbon trimmed in silver. She usually placed the delicate confection around the branches like a garland. Her finishing touch.

Spying the neatly coiled rolls of ribbon in a bin, she was

just reaching for one when she heard a car engine outside. It was too early for Rob to be home. She peeked out to spy a black-and-yellow taxi pulling into her driveway. She set down the ribbon and went to the foyer window for a better look. Then, to her shock, she watched a plumpish woman with long white hair and a multicolored poncho emerge from the vehicle. The driver helped the woman remove a zebra-striped rolling bag and a smaller hot pink leopard print one from the trunk. Smiling and laughing, the fellow helped the woman get her luggage up to the house. And then it hit Jane.

"Mother?" she said to herself in disbelief. What on earth was Lulu doing here?

Before she could gather her wits or call Rob with this distressing news, the doorbell was ringing. Wishing she could just ignore it, go into her room, lock the door, and hide, Jane slowly walked to the front door. Her ears were ringing and her pulse was racing as she opened the door.

"Wha—" She didn't even get the words out before Lulu grabbed her up into a bear hug.

"Oh, baby girl," she gushed. "I'm so glad to see you." She stepped back and patted Jane's cheek. "You look too thin, Moonbeam. And pale too. Have you been sick?"

Jane had no words, watching as Lulu paid the taxi driver, generously tipping him and thanking him for the "delightful drive," then looping the strap of her pink bag over one shoulder.

"It's darn cold out here," Lulu said as she wheeled her zebra bag past Jane into the foyer. "Do you think there'll be snow?"

Jane mutely shut the door, trying to understand what was happening.

"I haven't seen a white Christmas in ages," Lulu continued,

laughing. "But then again, no one does in San Diego." She looked around the house. "My, my, it looks like you've done some redecorating since my last visit. But it's been a while. Livvie's eighth-grade graduation, I think. That's been quite some time."

Lulu left her bags at the foot of the stairs and continued on through the house, commenting in her usual candid way about the decor. Of course, she didn't like anything . . . not that she said as much. But Jane had no doubts this was not Lulu's eccentric style. Finally they were in the kitchen, where Lulu made herself comfortable on a breakfast bar stool.

"I should've gotten a bite to eat on my way out here, but I was so eager to arrive, I came straight from the airport. I'm ravenous, Moonbeam. Got anything good to eat in this big ol' fancy kitchen?" Lulu kicked off her ankle-length fire-engine-red boots and stretched out her legs. "I'm going to have to do some tai chi before bed. I'm all tied up in knots."

"Mother?" Jane spoke slowly. "What are you doing here?"

Lulu let loose with that hearty belly laugh that Jane remembered from childhood, acting like life was so perfect—just a great big bowl of cherries—while it was really just a great big mess. "I'm here for Christmas, of course. What did you think?"

"I, uh, I don't know. But . . . uh, why? I mean, how did this happen?"

"Rob called last week and invited me."

"Last week?"

"Yeah, it was so sweet of him. How could I resist? It's been too long since I've seen my little Moonbeam and—"

"Please, Mother, do not call me Moonbeam. I go by Jane now. I think you are aware of that."

"Yes, yes. Jane. Plain Jane. Such a sad little name."

"I prefer it to—uh . . ." Jane couldn't bring herself to say the detestable childhood name aloud.

"I know, I know. But when I think about you, darling, and when I pray for you, I always call you Moonbeam. Cut an old lady some slack, okay?" Lulu winked. "A rose is a rose is a rose by any other name, right?"

Jane wasn't so sure.

Lulu held up her phone, and its bejeweled case sparkled in the pendant light above the breakfast bar. "How about I call for pizza. Do you have a place that delivers?"

"I don't really know. I don't eat pizza."

Lulu set down her phone. "Chinese?" she asked.

"Let me see if I can find something here," Jane told her. "I was going to make chicken for dinner, but I think I have some leftover green salad."

Lulu's smile faded. "Green salad?" She got up from the stool and went to the fridge. Opening it, she let out a dismal sigh. "Good grief, Moon—I mean, Jane. This looks like the cooler in an understocked health food store. Not that I don't appreciate healthy food. But don't you have anything hearty?" She pulled out a wedge of cheese, some deli turkey slices, and a couple other things. "Maybe some of this will brighten up a salad." She set some blue cheese out. "Can I make you something too?"

Jane shook her head, then watched in numb shock as Lulu rummaged through the fridge, pulling out all kinds of miscellaneous items and spreading the mess across the counter, chatting the whole time as if this was just another day and not a totally startling and unnerving event that was making Jane feel slightly sick to her stomach. All she could do was sit down and watch with morbid fascination. Sort of like watching a train wreck. When Lulu finished assembling a rather massive chef's salad in a small mixing bowl, Jane stood and began putting away her mom's debris.

"No, no, darling. Let me get that," Lulu insisted.

"It's okay. I'll get it."

"Well, whatever floats your boat." Lulu laughed. "Speaking of floating a boat, I don't think I told you about going rafting down the Colorado River a couple years ago." And although Jane had no interest, her mother launched into a detailed tale of a bunch of old people on a guided rafting trip and all the exciting things that went wrong. It was like Lulu relished the drama, but the whole thing made Jane feel even more on edge. Finally, as she was wiping the counters for the second time, her mother appeared to be done with her oversized chef salad. But instead of carrying her bowl to the sink and rinsing it, she left it where it was and began to walk about, seeming to thoroughly inspect Jane's remodeled kitchen. Was she going to offer a compliment?

"My goodness, Moonbeam, your kitchen certainly has everything, doesn't it!"

Cringing at the old name, Jane just shrugged. "As long as we were enlarging it . . ."

"And I mean everything *times two*." She shook her head in wonder. "Double ovens." She pulled out the top dishwasher drawer and then the bottom one. "And *two* dishwashers too? Goodness, you could probably prepare a royal feast in here. Do you entertain a lot?"

"Not a lot." Jane reached for her mom's salad bowl, rinsing it carefully before putting it in the dishwasher. She ignored her mother poking around and washed her hands with antiseptic soap. Just in case the fork and bowl were contaminated with germs. After all, her mother had just flown from San Diego, and everyone knew what a petri dish an airport could be. And her mother hadn't even washed her hands yet.

"How about having a big shindig for Christmas, Moon—I mean Jane," her mom caught herself. "I could help with the cooking. I've got some great recipes for the holidays and—"

"No, thank you." Jane put her used paper towel in the garbage compacter and leaned against the breakfast bar with her arms crossed. "We never have a big crowd at Christmas."

"What a shame, when you have such a perfectly lovely place to do it." She opened an upper cabinet. "And all these dishes too. I could never have glass doors on my cabinets. Too many mismatched and chipped dishes. But my guests never complain. I guess that's because they come for the fun of it. Not to admire how fancy things are." She ran a finger over the top of the quartz countertop. "Or how clean." She got closer to Jane, locking eyes with her. "Really, sweetheart, you should loosen up and have some friends over. Christmas is the perfect time for an open house."

Jane stepped back, nervously grabbing a spray bottle from beneath the sink and busying herself with cleaning her shiny countertops. "Well, uh, I don't think Rob likes a crowd of people in the house." Of course, this was a flat-out fib, but she couldn't seem to stop herself. "But Olivia will be here for Christmas."

Lulu clapped her hands. "Oh, the darling. I can't wait to see her. It's been too long since I've been here to see all of you."

Not long enough, Jane thought. And Christmas was still more than a week off. Did this mean she really had to endure her eccentric mother that entire time? What on earth had Rob been thinking when he'd invited her? And why hadn't he given her some warning? Perhaps she could've pretended to be gone or sick or something. Just wait until she got her hands on that man! Although she'd never been a violent person, Jane felt like that could change come six o'clock tonight. Rob had some explaining to do!

ten

OLIVIA HAD NEVER considered herself handy in the kitchen. She could've blamed it on her mother, and it wouldn't be untrue since Mom was always too persnickety in the kitchen to make culinary experimentation any fun. But in all fairness, she'd been on her own for long enough to have given it a try. So, really it was a personal choice. She just didn't really enjoy cooking. But maybe baking would be different.

She pulled out the sugar cookie recipe she'd googled on her phone and then carefully written out on the back of an envelope this morning. It seemed fairly simple and straightforward.

Olivia washed her hands and then stared at the ingredients she'd gotten on her way home from work. She'd left early with the intent to work at home, although she might have to catch up on that this weekend. But, all lined up on the small kitchen counter, the various baking items gave the impression that she knew what she was doing. Relieved that Tracie was still at work and planned to be late due to a holiday party, Olivia got out a mixing bowl. Fortunately, Tracie loved to cook and had a fully equipped albeit compact kitchen, complete with Christmas cookie cutters. Which was where Olivia had gotten the idea to make cookies in the first place.

With cheerful Christmas music playing on her phone, Olivia began to sing along as she followed the recipe's steps. Creaming the butter, eggs, and vanilla together, she thought about Malcolm. And, okay, she knew it was probably premature, but she was imagining herself in their kitchen, happily concocting yummy dishes. Perhaps doing the prep tasks together along with a glass of wine. It was a lovely image.

As she measured flour and other dry ingredients into a separate bowl, she wondered if her pipe dreams were just that—puffs of smoke. After all, she hadn't heard from Malcolm in almost a week. Although he had warned her when dropping her off after their uncomfortably quiet ride home that he'd be working long hours to compensate for the holiday vacation days he planned to take. So she'd been trying not to obsess over it.

Still, as she stirred the dry and wet ingredients together, she wasn't so sure. Despite her high hopes that Malcolm was the one, she knew that something about the past weekend had disturbed him. And she was pretty sure that something was her mom. But in the past few days, and after some good conversations with Tracie, who was going to make a terrific therapist when she got her license, Olivia had decided to convince Malcolm that she was not her mom—and that she never would be. Like Tracie had said, a future husband might assume that a girl would grow up to be her mother.

"It was a popular theory—that is, back in the Dark Ages," she'd assured Olivia. "And sure, I suppose there could be cases like that, but it's unfair to think it's a diehard rule."

And so Olivia had decided to make a pretty and hopefully

tasty platter of Christmas cookies to take to Malcolm while he was at work at the vet clinic. She would casually say it was to share with coworkers or pet owners or whatever. But hopefully it would give her an opportunity to (1) show him that she was not her mom, since her mom had never made Christmas cookies like this, claiming they were too messy, (2) show him that she still cared about him, and (3) ask him about sharing a ride home for Christmas. It seemed a perfect plan. No, no, not *perfect*! She hated that word. It was simply an idea that she hoped would remind him she was still around. And hopefully he hadn't written her off.

By the time the cookies were done and colorfully frosted and arranged on the platter she'd gotten just for this purpose, she knew they looked a little sloppy. The Santas were a blur of red and white, which started to resemble pink, the angels looked less than angelic, and the Christmas trees looked more like mossy trolls than trees. But as she put them in her car, she decided this could work in her favor since they were clearly not perfect. At least they were tasty.

She knew Malcolm had been working the night shift from three to midnight, so she knew he'd be there. But when she parked in front, she was dismayed not to see his SUV. *It's probably in the back*, she reminded herself, carefully getting out the cookie plate, resecuring the plastic wrap that had started to congeal with the still moist frosting. *Well, whatever*, she chuckled to herself. *Here's to imperfection.*

A brunette receptionist smiled from the front desk, glancing around behind Olivia. "Do you have a pet? Or are you delivering cookies?" She sounded hopeful.

"I was hoping to leave these with Dr. McEntire," Olivia said a bit formally.

"Oh?" The young woman stood, looking down at the cookies with a puzzled expression. Maybe she was trying to figure out if they were tainted. "Are you a client here?"

"No." Olivia laughed. "I don't have a pet. Just a personal friend. Is Malcolm here?"

Before the receptionist could answer, a woman with short gray hair wearing a pale green smock popped her head into the reception area.

"Cassie, can you call Mrs. Stillman and let her know her cat is going to have to stay for overnight observation?"

"You got it, Dr. Reiner." The receptionist reached for the phone. "And this woman is here to see Dr. McEntire. Is he back there?"

"No, I gave him the rest of his shift off."

"Lucky duck."

"Well, the poor boy's been working so hard this week. Two double shifts. He looked so tired I gave him the key to my beach cabin and told him to go relax for a couple days. He'll be pulling all night shifts next week until his holiday vacation time." The older woman peered curiously at Olivia.

"I, uh, just brought these Christmas cookies," Olivia said lamely. "For Malcolm. And to share with his coworkers. I guess I'll just leave them here." She set the platter on the counter.

"Did Dr. McEntire take Sadie to the beach with him?" the receptionist asked.

The vet grinned. "Are you kidding? Those two have been inseparable all week long. Ever since Sadie's mama died."

"Yeah, that was so sad to hear. Poor Sadie."

Olivia was backing up now but still listening.

"Well, Sadie really needs him," the receptionist continued.

"Yes. And I'm glad they can get away for some downtime."

The vet glanced at Olivia, who stood frozen by the door, taking this all in. *Who was Sadie?* "Thank you for the cookies," the vet said politely. "And we'll let Malcolm know you brought them when he gets back here."

"Although they might be gone by then." The receptionist had already peeled off some of the gooey plastic wrap and picked out a pink Santa. "Well, if they're any good."

"Oh, I think they're okay," Olivia assured her. "Taste better than they look. I'm not a very experienced baker, but the recipe I used had five stars."

The receptionist took a bite, then licked a finger and nodded eagerly. "Yum! They are good. Thanks!"

"Merry Christmas!" Olivia's smile felt stiff as she feigned enthusiasm she did not feel.

By the time she got into her car, she felt like crying. Could it be that in just one week's time, Malcolm not only had a new romantic prospect but was right now taking her to the coast for the weekend? Clearly, he was not the guy she thought he was.

She felt tears burning as she navigated commuter traffic to drive back to her apartment. Still, she told herself, it was better to find this out now than to learn of it later. At least she wouldn't be spending her holiday vacation wasting time on romantic imaginings. Yes, it hurt. More than she cared to admit—even to herself. But at least this gave her time to toughen up before going home next week. She had no doubts that Dad would ask questions about their relationship.

Thinking of Dad reminded her of the voicemail he'd left her this morning letting her know that Grandma Lulu had arrived a couple days ago and was already making her mother perfectly miserable with her messes. "The first step in our intervention plan," he'd said. And although she agreed it was a necessary step, she couldn't help but feel a bit guilty. It was always easier to feel sorry for Mom from a distance, but Olivia knew if she were home right now, she would feel differently.

She'd planned to call and cheer her dad and grandmother on this evening, but, knowing how close she was to breaking down in uncontrollable sobs, she'd have to wait. Hopefully her skin would thicken up in the next few days. In the meantime, she would try to forget about Malcolm and his Sadie girlfriend, whoever she was, if that was even possible.

eleven

LULU HAD ONLY BEEN a guest for three days—three excruciatingly long days—but by day two Jane felt she was losing her mind. Literally. Besides feeling foggy and confused, she was extremely irritable about everything. It didn't help that she and Rob were not speaking. Rather, *she* was not speaking to him. That stubborn man kept trying to make small talk, acting like nothing was wrong. But she was so infuriated with him, she couldn't even risk the slightest verbal exchange for fear she would explode into uncontrolled swearing. And she had never in her life uttered a single bad word and had always abhorred hearing others engage in such infantile behavior. But the words rolling through her head right now were profane enough to make a logger blush.

To make matters worse, Rob, who'd never seemed overly fond of his mother-in-law, seemed to be actually enjoying her company. Jane should've been grateful for the time the strange pair spent playing cribbage or watching ridiculous YouTube videos after dinner since it meant fewer interactions between her and her mom, plus it allowed her to sneak off to bed unnoticed. And yet their uncanny compatibility was like adding insult to injury and was profoundly aggravating.

On top of that, Lulu's insistence on "helping" in the kitchen had become the tipping point. If Jane was really going to lose it, her kitchen would be the battleground she would surely die upon. For the last three nights, her "helpful" mother had concocted all sorts of bizarre international dinners that Jane and Rob had never even heard of. Where she'd collected her strange ingredients was a mystery. Maybe they'd come in her zebra-striped bag. And whether or not it was to further torment Jane, who refused to eat her mom's awful food, Rob appeared to enjoy each feast that Lulu prepared and even offered to shop for her. But it was the messes Lulu left behind that really pushed Jane's buttons. It was like something from a bad dream, which was no exaggeration since nightmarish images of her ravaged kitchen woke her in the wee hours. Not that she was getting much sleep. Oh, she'd pretend to be snoozing after hurriedly setting her book aside before Rob came to bed. Never mind she'd reread the same chapter over and over.

At the sound of her husband's heavy treads outside the bedroom door, she'd turn off the bedside light and roll over. Then, keeping her breathing even to further convince Rob she was out, she waited for him to complete his nighttime routine in the bathroom, slowly counting in her head. Since he wasn't very meticulous about personal hygiene, she rarely counted to two hundred before he rolled into bed, and later she'd discover in his haste he'd left the toilet seat up, which really peeved her.

Rob didn't normally use the master bath since it was an unspoken rule that it was more her domain. But having a guest in the house made him abandon his regular use of the hall bath. Just one more irksome detail of this severe form of holiday internment. That's what it felt like—like being a prisoner in her own home with insufferable guards intent on driving her over the edge. And the edge was close!

She wasn't sure if Rob or Lulu were aware of how she'd get up late at night after the house was quiet and she felt confident they were asleep. She'd sneak out of bed and into the kitchen for a deep-cleaning session. Sure, the midnight chore made her more tired and cranky the next day, but it also brought her a semblance of peace. Or at least that's what she told herself. To be honest, peace felt as remote as Mars right now.

On the fourth morning of Lulu's never-ending visit, Jane called her hairdresser for a pre-Christmas appointment and the potential for escape. She knew she should've done this days ago, but life had been too upside down for her to think rationally, and when Phoebe at the hair salon said she was booked until after Christmas, Jane felt her spirits tumble even lower. Quite honestly, she didn't enjoy having her hair done in a salon—it always made her uncomfortable as it was too public, with too many onlookers. For that reason, Phoebe had talked her into buying the bluing solution she used to keep Jane's hair sparkling platinum instead of the rather tarnished brassy shade it looked today. Jane had only used this magical blue solution a couple of times to touch up her hair between appointments, but the process was fairly simple and the results well worth the effort. And right now, her hair color was detestable.

So when Rob offered to take her mother Christmas shopping in the afternoon, Jane felt almost ecstatic. Okay, that was a stretch. But the thought of having her whole house entirely to herself was surprisingly gratifying. And it provided the perfect time of privacy to get her hair into better shape for the holidays. Perhaps she'd even give herself a clay mask facial. This would be her "be kind to Jane" afternoon.

She'd been surprised Rob was willing to leave his office for the whole afternoon just to take Lulu on a Christmas shopping adventure, which Jane could only imagine but didn't want to, so good riddance to both of them! Humming to herself, Jane set to work in her master bath. First, she locked the door—just in case—then she went ahead and applied her favorite mask to her face. She usually gave it about fifteen minutes before showering. While the mask did its work, she carefully covered her marble countertop with kraft paper to prevent any blue stains. She lined up the necessary ingredients: a bottle of cobalt blue dye, gloves, the comb she kept especially for the blue dye, a plastic shower cap to cover her hair for the five minutes it took for the dye to soak in, and a timer. Next, she got her shower set up with plenty of navy towels laid out here and there to use for wiping up just in case the dye splashed while rinsing. She wished she'd brought her phone in here to put on her favorite classical music, but maybe silence was better.

She stripped down to be ready for her shower, put on her black shortie robe she had for this very purpose and some protective gloves, and then began to apply the dye, carefully combing it through her hair. The first time Phoebe had recommended the bluing solution, Jane had been skeptical. She remembered Mrs. Barnes, her first-grade teacher. The elderly woman had curly white hair that went from shades of blue to lavender to pink every couple of weeks. Jane certainly hadn't wanted to look like that. But Phoebe had said it would brighten her hair and subdue any yellowing of the gray, turning it more platinum. And Jane had loved how her hair was sparkly and shiny after she was done. She'd only done it herself a few times, but the results were always surprisingly pleasant.

After the dark blue dye was liberally applied and combed through, Jane set the timer for five minutes. She knew the solution could stay on as long as ten minutes, but she stuck with five, preferring to err on the side of caution. And then she sat down on the toilet seat and picked up the December issue of *House Beautiful*. Maybe it would inspire her to finish decorating her house for Christmas.

But she'd barely opened the glossy magazine when she noticed a large black spider crawling up the wall right next to her. Jumping up, she grabbed a clump of toilet tissue and attempted to nail the invader before it got high enough to make messy cobwebs on the ceiling. But the critter was fast and quickly climbed out of reach, so she stepped onto the lid of the toilet seat in an attempt to nab it, and she suddenly felt the seat giving way beneath.

The next thing she knew, she had her left leg in the toilet, and with her legs splayed like an acrobat, her right hip was in unimaginable pain. The pain was so intense, she didn't actually remember how she got her leg out of the toilet and herself onto the floor, but she knew that getting off the floor, thanks to whatever had happened to her hip, was excruciatingly impossible. The timer went off, and she curled on the hard tile floor in an almost fetal position, in severe pain and sobbing "My hair! My hair!" over and over again.

twelve

THE THICK, heavy clouds hovering over the mountain pass looked foreboding, but Olivia wasn't concerned. She'd grown up on the snowy side of the Cascades and was used to driving in this climate, and fortunately she'd already had her winter tires put on. In fact, she was hoping for snow this Christmas. So it wasn't weather worries that were gnawing at her right now. She turned off the Christmas music she'd put on to cheer her up during the drive home and allowed herself to sort out her thoughts.

First and foremost, she told herself, she should be concerned for her mother. According to Dad, she'd taken a bad fall and now had a fractured hip. He hadn't gone into the details of how it happened, and hadn't asked her to come earlier than planned, but she could hear the strain in his voice.

"It's not as serious as it sounds," he'd reassured her. "According to the ER doctor, hips heal slowly, but with physical therapy they do get better. Mostly she needs to avoid putting pressure on it for a month or so to allow it to heal, but apparently she also needs to be somewhat mobile to heal it."

"No pressure and somewhat mobile. What does that mean?"

"It means she'll be sedentary most of the time and using a walker to get around."

"Is she in pain?"

"She's got meds."

"Is she still in the hospital?"

"Just overnight. She can come home tomorrow."

"And then what?" Olivia knew her grandmother was there but wasn't sure how Mom would handle being nursed by her.

"I really don't know, honey. Anyway, I need to go back and check on her." He cleared his throat. "She's, uh, having a bad hair day." Then he'd sort of laughed.

Olivia wasn't sure what to make of that, but she'd decided then and there that her holiday vacation would start in the morning. She wasn't sure how this new development would affect their intervention plan. Maybe a broken hip was God's way of intervening. But she knew she wouldn't find out until she got there and assessed the situation.

Mom's hip wasn't the only problem troubling her, but the other thing was too hard to think about. Every time she replayed the idea of Malcolm and Sadie spending the weekend at some cozy beach cabin hideaway, she wanted to scream . . . or just cry. And so she was refusing to think about it. At least, that's what she told herself. But all the while it kept niggling at her. Like a little tormentor determined to get her attention.

"Just get over it! Move on!" she scolded herself. "Malcolm obviously has."

As simple as that sounded, she knew it wasn't easy. And since she still had almost an hour before she'd be home, she decided to just get it out of her system, walking through every memory that seemed to haunt her, until she reached the last conversation they'd had. And sure, he'd explained how he'd taken on double shifts in order to get good holiday vacation time. But had he really done that to get some vacation time at the beach with Sadie? Or was she just getting paranoid about nothing?

She tried to remember the tone of his voice in that last brief conversation. She wanted to convince herself it was apologetic, but in hindsight, it had been rather abrupt. She'd attributed it to him being overworked and tired. But maybe it was something more. Maybe he was trying to send her the subtle message he was done with her.

And why shouldn't he be? After all, their families were like the Hatfields and McCoys, or the Capulets and Montagues, or whatever . . . and to be fair, it wasn't Malcolm's family that was to blame. It was all her mom. But it was hard to be mad at Mom when she was suffering so. Still, it probably wouldn't improve neighborly relations between the Bradshaws and McEntires.

Like a dog chasing its tail, Olivia continued to grapple with these conflicting thoughts as she pulled into her parents' driveway. "Let it go," she told herself as she got out of her car and stretched. It was time to be a good daughter and focus on her mother. As she tugged her bag out of her trunk, Dad appeared.

"Let me take that," he told her. "You go in and see your mom. She's looking forward to it."

"Okay." She kissed his cheek.

"And please don't laugh at her."

"Laugh?" She blinked. "Why on earth would I laugh at her?"

His expression was hard to read. "You'll see."

Even before Olivia went inside, she could see the influence of her wacky grandmother, from the bright-colored Snoopy and Red Baron wreath on the glossy black door to the mat on the front step that said "Welcome Gnome" and was adorned with little red and green gnomes. Probably a good thing her mom wasn't mobile yet. The inside of the house was even worse. Or better, depending on how you looked at it. Where her mother's taste was cool elegance, Grandma Lulu preferred goofiness and silliness. She was a woman who loved to laugh and make things light and merry—which went well with Christmas. In fact, in many ways she was very much like the neighbors Olivia's mother detested.

Lulu's touch included multicolored lights and flashy garlands draped all about Mom's angel display to make it even brighter. The tree that was still partially decorated with her mom's crystal was now overwhelmed with funny tacky ornaments. As she set her bag on a chair, Olivia wondered where on earth Lulu had managed to gather all these weird trinkets.

"Hello, hello." Lulu emerged from the kitchen wearing a Santa hat and a twinkling necklace that looked like it was made out of mini Christmas tree lights. "My darling granddaughter has arrived! Merry Christmas, sweetie pie." She embraced Olivia in a big bear hug. "And not a minute too soon."

"How's it going?" Olivia asked. "How's Mom?"

"She's only been home about an hour, but she's mad as a wet hen."

"Uh-huh?" Olivia peeled off her coat.

"She's trying not to show it." Lulu lowered her voice as she motioned her into the kitchen. "But if her scowl gets any darker, it'll probably be so deeply carved into her face that her Botox won't even help."

Olivia's eyes opened wide as she took in the kitchen. She'd never seen it like this before. Cluttered counters, dirty dishes in the sink, miscellaneous groceries everywhere, cabinet doors hanging open, and more gaudy Christmas garlands and interesting items spread all about.

"I see you've been decorating for Christmas." Olivia flipped the Santa sled and reindeer mobile suspended between the brass pendant lights over the breakfast bar. "Did you bring all these things from San Diego?"

"No, no." Lulu waved her hand. "Your dad took me to the dollar store to shop yesterday. My goodness, it's a treasure trove there. I brought home bags and bags. Of course, that was before we knew your poor mother had fallen and hurt herself. But I stayed up late last night decorating. I thought it would cheer her up when she got home this morning."

"And did it?" Olivia could just imagine!

"Well, she looked surprised. She didn't say much as your dad wheeled her in. She's got a wheelchair, you know. And I guess the trip home must've worn her out. She just wanted to go to her room to rest. Probably due to the pain meds."

"Uh-huh." Olivia wanted to add that the pain meds were probably helping her mom not totally flip out over the state of her home. "Should I go check on her? Or do you think she's asleep? What can I do to help?"

"She might be asleep. I was just fixing her a lunch tray since she hasn't eaten since breakfast, and according to your dad, she barely touched that." Lulu spread a Santa placemat on a tray. "Maybe you can take it to her."

"Okay." Olivia watched as Lulu set a greasy-looking grilled cheese sandwich on a plate, along with a small dish of cottage cheese. Then, using canned whipped cream, she created a small white mound on what looked like cocoa steaming in a Rudolph mug. Probably another dollar store find. "That's a lot of dairy."

"Calcium is important for healing bones."

Olivia noticed the jug of whole milk still on the counter. "Mom usually has nonfat milk. I mean, when she has it, which is rarely."

"Pishposh." Lulu wrinkled her nose. "Everyone knows that whole milk products are better for us." She folded a bright red-and-green paper napkin to set on the tray and smiled. "Ta-da, there you go. Want to take that in to her? She'll be so happy to see you."

Olivia nodded as she picked up the tray but felt fairly certain her mother would not be happy to see this lunch.

"Try to get her to eat," Lulu urged. "I've noticed she eats like a bird, and it's obvious that she's underweight. That hip isn't going to heal without good nutrition and calcium. And, by the way, don't laugh at her."

Olivia frowned. "Why is everyone saying that?"

Lulu just tossed back her head and let out a hearty chuckle. "Oh, you'll see." She patted Olivia on the back. "You'll see."

Olivia was speechless when she saw her mother's bright blue hair poking out beneath a loosely tied cream-colored scarf.

"Mom," she said as she set the tray on the bedside table. "I'm so sorry about your hip." She leaned down to kiss her cool, pale cheek. "How are you doing?"

"Oh, Olivia, I'm so glad you came." And Jane began to cry.

Olivia pulled a nearby chair closer, sitting down to be at her mom's level. "Are you in pain?"

"I've never felt more miserable in my life. Even giving birth to you was better than this."

"Really?" Olivia blinked. She'd heard the horror story of her mom giving birth . . . and why she'd decided one child was plenty.

"I feel like I'm being punished." Jane reached for a Kleenex.

Olivia put a hand on her mom's shoulder. "I'm so sorry, Mom. What can I do to help?"

"Get your grandmother out of my house?" Jane narrowed her eyes. "I can't stand it, Olivia. She's driving me absolutely nuts."

Olivia didn't know what to say, so she changed topics by asking how Mom hurt her hip, listening as she blubbered a nonsensical story about a spider and how she was putting blue on her hair and fell down.

"I was stuck on the bathroom floor for hours," she finally said, pausing to blow her nose.

Olivia touched a strand of periwinkle hair. "And that rinse was on too long . . . and turned your hair, uh, blue?"

"Yes." Jane looked up with red-rimmed eyes. "Is there anything you can do about it?"

"I don't know anything about hair dyes, Mom. But I'm guessing it's going to be like that for a while." She pulled out her phone. "Want me to do some research to see if there's a remedy? Or I could call your hairdresser and ask her."

"Yes, yes," Jane said eagerly. "Please, do something."

"I'll make you a deal." Olivia put the tray on Mom's lap. "You try and eat something, and I'll see what I can find out."

"Ugh. This looks repulsive."

"I don't know." Olivia picked up a sandwich half and sniffed it. "You used to make these for me when I was little. Remember? Along with tomato soup. It was one of my favorite snowy day lunches." She grinned. "Want me to taste it to make sure it's alright?"

Jane just shrugged, watching with arched brows as Olivia took a bite.

"Oh, Mom, it's yummy. I can tell there are several kinds of cheese in here. You have to try it. I'm going to ask Grandma to make me one just like it."

Jane made a *humph* sound but picked up the other half. "Probably a thousand calories in it." But she took a tiny bite and slowly chewed.

Meanwhile, Olivia picked up her phone and began to hunt for remedies for overly dyed hair. Unfortunately, it wasn't looking too promising, but as her mom slowly ate, she read the suggestions aloud. Everything from olive oil to salt and vinegar.

"Sounds like salad," she joked. "And this one says wash over and over with strong dish soap and follow with lots of conditioner." She glanced at her sad-looking mom. "It'll be hard to do much of this with you incapacitated like you are, but I can try to help you if you want."

Jane nodded eagerly as she chewed. "Yes, please do. I can't bear to look like this. It's bad enough to be convalescing at Christmas, but blue hair too. Throw Lulu into the mix and, really, Olivia, I feel like I'm in some kind of personal prison."

Olivia gave her a sympathetic pat on the shoulder before taking a better peek at the mop of blue beneath the silk scarf. It really did look hopeless. But if this was God's way of intervening, it was certainly more effective than anything they could've cooked up.

"You finish your lunch, and I'll try to figure out a way to help with your hair." She looked at the nearby wheelchair, wondering how easy it would be to get that to the shower, where she could lean her mom's head back and do the rinsing with the handheld shower head. "You could always just cut it," she suggested. "Or wear a stocking hat. Or dye it black."

"Or shave it all off and wear a wig," Jane said glumly. "But where do you find a good wig a week before Christmas?"

"A lot of people dye their hair bright colors just for the fun of it." Olivia had never personally wanted lime green or purple hair, but it looked good on other people. "You can be very avant-garde and chic for your age group."

"Please." Jane rolled her eyes. "Let's try some of those remedies you just read to me. And in the meantime, please refrain from calling me Mama Smurf like the ER nurse did yesterday."

Olivia couldn't help but giggle at that one and, to her surprise, her mother almost smiled. "Well, we'll just make the best of it." She tried to sound positive. "After we try those remedies, I think you should just style as usual and maybe it'll grow on you. Blue has always been your favorite color."

Jane's response was a guttural moan. But Olivia thought her mother, now sporting Smurf-blue hair, might be perfectly set up to stop taking life so seriously. After all, Christmas was supposed to be a season of merrymaking, goodness, and joy—and heaven knew they all needed to laugh more.

thirteen

JUST WHEN JANE thought life couldn't get worse, Cindy from next door dropped in with a plate of cookies. Her neighbor rarely graced her home since Jane had given her clear signals long ago that she was not particularly welcome. Oh, she'd never been exactly rude about it, but her consistent chilly reception had provided a pretty decent clue. And it had seemed to work. Jane's way of showing her appreciation was to never shadow her neighbor's doorstep and expect that Cindy would continue to do likewise. But Lulu apparently didn't understand these unwritten neighborhood rules. Hearing the two women merrily chattering away right now was more than a little disturbing.

It was only Jane's second day of recovering after her embarrassing fall, and she was yet to emerge from the safe sanctity of her bedroom, but she could hear Cindy and Lulu's voices easily through her open door. If she'd been able, she would've jumped up from her bed and closed and locked her door, but so far, she'd only been up a few times to use the toilet, and only with Olivia's help.

But Olivia was out running errands right now. Hopefully, among other things, to secure an attractive wig to conceal Jane's horrid hair. All of Olivia's home remedies had only managed to tone the blue down a few shades and turn her hair into a straw-like texture. So now instead of looking like a wannabe teenager, she resembled an old lady who had used a bit too much blue on her scarecrow-like hair. It was just plain ugly. And at the moment, she had neither a scarf nor a hat on hand to hide her shame.

"Go on in and say hello," Lulu was telling Cindy. "Take your cookies in for her to see. They're so pretty and yet delicious. Honestly, I can't believe you baked them yourself."

"I love making Christmas cookies." Cindy's voice sounded as if they were right outside her doorway now. "Are you sure I'm not disturbing her?"

"No, she'll be glad to see you," Lulu assured her.

Jane tried to slump down in her bed, grabbing a pillow to hide her hair, but it was too late. Cindy was already walking up to her bedside, looking down with eyes filled with pity. Of course, she had no idea that Jane despised being pitied. She much preferred being admired or even envied. But never pitied. Still, it was too late to hide. And so she simply folded her arms in front of her and glowered at the intrusive neighbor.

"I'm sorry to barge in," Cindy glanced at Lulu. "But your mother said it was—"

"I heard what my mother said," Jane snapped. "Thank you for the cookies. Please take them to the kitchen." She stopped herself from adding "and put them in the trash compactor."

"I was so sorry to hear of your injury," Cindy continued as if oblivious to her unwanted presence. "If there's anything I can do to help, I hope you'll call. You know that's what neighbors are for—to help each other when in need."

"Thank you, but my daughter and mother are more than enough help. And Rob as well."

Cindy was staring at her hair now. "That was unfortunate about your hair. Rob told Erik all about it. I was so sorry for you. You have such gorgeous hair normally. I always wish my hair could have grayed and whitened as nicely as yours." She patted her short charcoal-gray hair. "But at least I have hair." She chuckled.

"Lucky you," Jane said dryly. She wanted to add that if Olivia didn't find an appropriate wig, she might have her daughter shave her head and wear hats until it grew out. Maybe she could pass herself off as a cancer survivor, although that seemed like a terrible way to conceal her stupidity.

Cindy noticed a scarf on a nearby chair but out of reach of the bed. "Have you been wearing scarves to cover your hair?" She picked it up. "This is really pretty."

"Yes. Olivia forgot to help me with that this morning."

"Why don't you let me?" Cindy set her cookie plate on the bureau and came over. "I used to be pretty good at this. Back when I had my chemo treatments. Thank God that's behind me now."

Jane blinked. "Did you have cancer?"

"Yes." She pointed to her chest. "I had a double. But I've been in remission for almost ten years now." She gently set the pale lavender scarf on top of Jane's head.

"Oh?" Jane felt a wave of guilt. "I, uh, I didn't know."

"Well, I didn't go around advertising." She began winding the scarf around Jane's hair. "I've always preferred these cotton scarves. Silky ones just slide right off my hair. I liked wearing them like a turban, because it gave more bulk to my head, which resembled a cue ball." She chuckled as she tied and tucked in the ends of the scarf. Then she picked up a hand mirror from the bedside table. "There. What do you think?"

Jane stared in wonder. "It looks perfect. Thanks."

Cindy patted her shoulder. "You're so beautiful, Jane, you make it look perfect."

Jane didn't know what to say, but she felt something like tears stinging behind her eyes. "Thank you," she muttered.

"Now, I won't bother you anymore," Cindy said, "if you try just one cookie." She pointed to the powdery white ones. "These are my favorites. Russian tea cakes. It's an old family recipe. But you might want a cup of tea or coffee with it." She picked up an empty tea mug from the bedside table. "How about I bring you some?"

Jane just mutely nodded. But while Cindy was getting her tea, she was assaulted by a big wave of guilt. Why had she been so hateful to Cindy? And why didn't she know she had gone through cancer treatments . . . why hadn't Rob told her? Unless he, too, was unaware. She knew there was no way to make up for past wrongs. She wasn't even sure she knew how to or if it was humanly possible. But at least she could try.

Cindy returned with a steaming cup of tea. "Here you go, dear. Lulu said this was your favorite one. I'm not much of a tea drinker, but it smells good."

"Thank you."

"Well, I'll leave you to it. I've got a long list of holiday chores today. Oh, I shouldn't call them chores since I enjoy them so much. But I better get going." She clasped Jane's shoulder. "I hope and pray your hip mends quickly. And honestly, if there's anything I can do, please let me know. That's what neighbors are for."

"Yes, thank you." Jane's smile was weak. "And I'll try to become a better neighbor." She felt insincere, but under the circumstances . . .

Cindy's dark eyes sparkled. "That's wonderful, Jane. Thank you so much. Now you take care." She blew a kiss as she left, and Jane, feeling satisfied that she'd taken a baby step toward becoming a better neighbor, leaned back with a sigh. Oh, she knew it would be easy to fall back into her old ways, but she would try to change.

For the next couple of days, Jane felt like the great pretender. Despite Olivia's inability to secure a wig, she acted like it was no big deal. After all, her family was getting used to the weird Mama Smurf hair. And wearing a headscarf was rather elegant, wasn't it? And when she told Rob to cancel their Christmas plans to host several prominent couples like they usually did—her big chance to get people to admire her home and holiday decor—she blamed it on her injury, not the truth that she was too embarrassed to have them see her like this.

And for the most part she was able to conceal her pain and humiliation as she sat in her wheelchair or hobbled about with her walker, feeling like she was about a hundred years old. She even managed to appear unaffected by the cheap, cheesy Christmas decorations spread through her home like a tasteless pestilence. And she even did her best to eat the food served to her without complaining. Thankfully, Olivia was doing some of the cooking now.

But by day five of her hip injury, she was inwardly seething and feeling like a pot about to boil over, and she wasn't sure how much longer she could contain it.

"Are you okay, Mom?" Olivia asked as she helped her get ready for the day.

"I'm fine," she snapped in a tone that clearly said she wasn't fine.

"It's okay to get angry about your situation," Olivia said as she slipped a loose tunic top over Jane's head.

"I'm *not* angry." Jane tugged at the elastic waist of the detestable purple knit pants. She'd been forced to wear these baggy things due to her injury. She had no idea where Olivia had found them, but as soon as she could get into real trousers, these ugly things would relocate to the trash. Thanks to her hip, she'd even been sleeping in these horrid pants.

"Okay." Olivia backed off with a skeptical expression. "Anything else I can help you with this morning?"

"No, thank you," she said curtly.

"Sure you don't want to get out of bed? I can help you into your wheelchair."

"Thanks, but no thanks." Jane leaned back into her bed.

Olivia just nodded, moving toward the door. "Let me know if you change your mind about getting out of here."

"I'm fine!" Jane exclaimed. "Please, stop hovering."

"Grandma will have your breakfast—"

"I don't want breakfast!" Jane yelled. "All I want is for everyone to leave me alone."

"Okay." Olivia held up her hands in surrender.

"And I want my house to return to my house," Jane continued hotly. It felt like something inside of her had snapped, like the woman she'd been trying to be had gone up in smoke and the real Jane was back. "I want all those trashy decorations removed. I want it all to be like it was before. I hate what you've all done. I hate everything about my life. I hate it, I hate it, I hate it." And she began to cry.

"Oh, Mom." Olivia came closer.

"No!" Jane looked up at her with tears streaming. "And I hate your pity. Please, just leave me alone. Tell everyone to just leave me alone. And for the record, I'm canceling Christmas this year."

Olivia's eyes were wide, but she mutely nodded.

"Oh, I don't care if the rest of you celebrate," Jane retreated a bit. "Just leave me out of it. And leave me alone."

"I'll tell Dad and Grandma that you need some alone time," Olivia said solemnly.

"Thank you," Jane growled. "And close the door."

Olivia did as she was told, but as soon as Jane was alone, she felt guilty. Why was she being so mean? What was wrong with her? Was there any hope? Right now, if she had a magic wand and could turn her home into what it used to be, what it normally was at Christmas, she thought perhaps she'd be happy. Except there was her aching hip and her immobility and her horrid blue hair to deal with. No, it was useless. She was right to want to cancel Christmas. In a way, it seemed Christmas had canceled itself. So be it!

fourteen

BY THE TIME he was driving home, Malcolm had heard a brief accounting of life on the home front from his mom. Of course, he wanted to hear the family news about his siblings and their families. Sounded like they were all fairly busy with miscellaneous holiday activities and Christmas programs, his dad finishing up birdhouses, his mom baking up a storm. Pretty much the norm for this time of year. However, he was surprised to hear about Mrs. Bradshaw's injured hip and even something about blue hair. But maybe there was a blessing in there somehow. Would it help that woman to get over herself and her perfectionist ways and give up her unrealistic expectations of everyone? Or was it beyond hope?

But these musings weren't what troubled him as he drove into his hometown. He glanced at the dog carrier buckled in the seat next to him. "Good girl, Sadie," he said gently. "You're a good traveler." As he drove into his neighborhood, his mind was on Olivia. She'd probably assumed he'd given up on her. Had he really? Sure, he'd wrestled with himself over the family dilemma, but then he'd gotten so buried in work at the clinic. From cats ingesting pine needles and poinsettias to overweight dogs sneaking into holiday cookie plates, they'd treated more than their normal share of clients. And Dr. Reiner had reminded him there would be lots more coming, considering the way people overindulged their poor animals at Christmastime. His already busy life seemed to be on steroids since he'd adopted poor Sadie. But he'd felt so sorry for the mixed breed pup after it was impossible to save her two littermates and sick mama. A homeless man had rescued them, dropping them at the clinic in a cardboard box. After caring for the surviving pup night and day—and naming her Sadie—Malcolm knew she'd be his for the duration of her life.

As he parked in his parents' driveway, he wondered how Olivia felt about dogs. He knew he'd neglected her this past week. And he had no doubt she'd noticed it. He'd heard about the weird Christmas cookies she'd dropped at the clinic, but by the time he was back in the office, they'd all been consumed and, according to the receptionist, they tasted better than they looked. He'd meant to send Olivia a little thank-you text, and he'd even tried to write one, but it had sounded so trite and dismissive that he'd canceled before sending. But, seeing her little car parked at her parents' house, he was assaulted by guilt, realizing this was something he'd need to fix in person. But not yet. He wanted to get Sadie settled in and see his family first.

As usual, his house looked and felt a bit chaotic when he went inside. But this wasn't the usual type of happy, noisy chaos. Oh, sure, there was the normal messiness of clutter in the living room and brightly colored Christmas decorations. And the dining room was strewn with holiday wrapping paper and ribbons and half-wrapped packages. But as he approached the kitchen, expecting to discover Mom pulling out a sheet of freshly baked cookies, instead of sweetness and spice, his nose was assaulted by a very foul smell. Worse than when the clinic kennels needed a thorough cleaning. Going inside, he saw soggy pink bath towels spread across the floor and his dad flat on his back with his head inside the opened sink cabinet.

"Dad!" He knelt down. "Are you okay?"

Erik slid out, pushing himself to a sitting position on the floor, a wrench in his hand and a frustrated frown on his face.

"What's up?" Malcolm gave him a hand, helping him to his feet.

"You mean besides sewage?" Dad's frown turned into a scowl as he wiped his hands on his jeans.

"Serious plumbing problems?"

"Not sure how serious they are. I'm not a plumber. Not much of a handyman either." Dad scrunched his nose. "Man, can you smell that?"

"Hard to miss." Malcolm set the pet carrier on the counter.

"I thought it was the kitchen sink. Your mom thought the drain was running slow, so I opened up the trap and water went everywhere." He looked at the towels spread about. "Guess I better get Mom's favorite towels off the floor before she comes back from the store."

"So did you fix it?" Malcolm took a peek under the sink, but, like Dad, he wasn't a plumber either.

"Nope." He pointed to the standing water in the sink. "I already tried running water there, and no go." Erik scratched his head. "I was hoping to figure it all out before your mom got home. But I guess I should try to call the plumber again."

Malcolm began to walk about the kitchen, sniffing, then

followed the foul aroma and a trail of water to the mudroom bath next to the laundry room. He opened the door to see the small bath was flooded, and it smelled so bad he pulled up his jacket to cover his nose. "Dad," he yelled. "You gotta see this."

Erik hurried in, letting out a loud moan. "Oh, crud. I should've known. But I didn't even think about this bathroom."

"You better get a plumber here. Fast."

"Yeah, this is definitely above my pay grade."

"Mine too." Malcolm backed up, trying not to breathe. "Aren't you supposed to shut off the water when you're having a plumbing problem?"

"Yeah, I did that after I made a mess with the kitchen sink drain."

"I'll help you clean this up." Malcolm unzipped his jacket as they headed for the kitchen.

Erik stopped by the laundry room, grabbing up an armful of towels and dropping them on the floor as they walked. "Go get a mop and a bucket or two," he instructed.

Malcolm removed his coat and rolled up his sleeves. "Think we need hazmat suits?"

"Probably."

As Erik called several plumbers who all seemed too busy to help, Malcolm gathered cleaning tools, and, slowly and stinkily, the two of them attempted to clean up the mess. As they wrung towels into buckets, they kicked around possible causes for the plumbing disaster. Finally, in the mudroom bath, Erik arrived at a possibility.

"Since it seems to have originated in here with both the toilet and bath flooding and not draining, and since this bathroom is the closest to our septic tank, I'm guessing that's the trouble."

"You're still on a septic tank?" Malcolm wrung out a filthy towel. "I thought the city ran sewer on this end of town back when I was in college."

"They did, but since we weren't annexed, we had the option to hook up or remain on our own systems for a period of time."

"A period of time?"

"Yeah, I can't remember the exact rules. And I always meant to get us hooked up, but . . . well, your mom got sick . . . life got busy. I guess I sort of forgot."

"Sounds like you need to get someone here to empty it, pronto." Malcolm grimaced at his hands. "And we really need some fresh water to clean ourselves up."

"But I turned off the water. And why turn it back on when we don't have drains?"

"Right now, we need to sanitize this place. And that'll take water and bleach. I can make a solution, like we use in the kennels, to make it all clean and safe. And we need it done before any of the kids come by."

"And since our house is Grand Central, that could happen in any given moment."

"I'm on it," Malcolm said.

"All this with Christmas less than a week away." Erik grimly shook his head. "Your poor mom."

"I'll grab some buckets and go next door to see if we can get some water from the Bradshaws' for cleanup," Malcolm said.

Erik was rummaging beneath the sink. "I think there's some hand sanitizer down here left over from the start of Covid. That might help us temporarily. But you better not go inside the Bradshaws' house. Jane will have a fit if she gets a whiff of you."

"I'll call Olivia first and give a heads-up." As Malcolm went for his phone, he wondered what kind of reception he'd get there. Olivia might not be happy to hear from him, and then to go over, smelling like this and begging for water? Maybe he could just use their hose. But what about a shower? And all these filthy towels? And Dad was right, it was impossible dealing with all this right before Christmas.

As he walked past Sadie's little dog crate, still sitting on the kitchen counter, he felt sorry for her containment, but didn't think it was safe for her to be let out before the floors were disinfected. What a mess! Even though he'd used the sanitizer, he handled his phone gingerly.

"Malcolm?" Olivia's voice sounded surprised, but perhaps also pleased? Hopefully.

"Hey, Olivia, how are you?" He waited for her polite albeit slightly cool reply, then launched into his parents' dilemma and how they needed water ASAP. "We could just use your hose if it's hooked up, but it would be nice to have some hot water too."

"Oh, Malcolm, that's horrible. No, you don't have to use the hose." She paused. "But maybe come around back and use the deep sink in the laundry room. My mom's in the living room right now . . . and not having the best day."

"Thanks. I'll bring some buckets."

By the time he got there, she was on the back step to meet him. "Come on in. I didn't mention your plumbing troubles to my mom. She's already stressing enough."

"I heard about her hip." He set the first bucket in the laundry sink. "Tell her I'm sorry and I hope it mends quickly." He glanced at Olivia, realizing, not for the first time, how pretty she was with her auburn hair and green eyes. Same coloring as her dad, but with the classic beauty of her mother.

"Your bucket is overflowing." She reached past him to turn off the tap.

"Oh, I guess I was distracted." He lifted the heavy bucket and set it down, then put the other one in the sink. "I wasn't prepared for coming home to a house that smelled like a septic tank." He looked down at himself. "I bet I stink too. Sorry."

"No, you're fine. But if you need a shower, or your dad does, come on over."

"But your mom—"

"Don't worry about her. This house has three bathrooms." Her mouth twisted to one side like she was thinking. "And you know, my grandma is using the sofa bed in Mom's craft room since she doesn't like stairs, so there's an empty spare bedroom upstairs if you or someone in your family needs it."

Malcolm felt his brows arch. "You think your mom won't mind?"

She reached to turn off the faucet again. "If she does mind, it'll be good for her." As he rinsed and washed his hands with real soap, she relayed how her family was trying to do an intervention for her mother's persnickety ways.

"Looks like God and nature are helping out with that." He set the second bucket down and glanced around the attractive and well-organized laundry room. "Man, Olivia, this laundry room looks like a spread from a fancy home decor magazine."

She shrugged. "You know my mom."

He ran a hand over an oak cabinet. "Pretty nice for a laundry room."

"Mom had those recycled from her kitchen remodel. Some in here and some in the garage."

"Well, I have to give it to your mom, she knows how to organize. My mom could use a little help in that regard."

"Too bad they don't get along better," she said. "They could compensate for each other's weaknesses."

"Wouldn't that be something."

"Well, as long as your mom was more influential than my mom. I love your mom." Her eyes widened. "Oh, I love my mom too," she said quickly. "I mean, I don't love how she does things, or how she treats, uh, some people. But I do love her. Although I must admit that seeing her going through the wringer right now is pretty amusing." As she walked him to the door, she told him about the spider her mom was trying to kill and about the blue hair until they were both laughing so hard some water slopped out of a bucket.

"Sorry."

"No worries. I'll get it." She patted his back. "Good luck with your plumbing woes. And really, you guys are welcome to shower over here. You can use my bathroom. And I'll hold back my mom." She laughed. "Actually, she'd need help to get up from her wheelchair, so I wouldn't even need to."

"Hey." He paused in the doorway. "One more thing. If I did stay here, I, uh, have a puppy in my care." He quickly explained about Sadie.

"So that's the mysterious Sadie." Her expression was hard to read. Was she relieved or amused? "I heard about Sadie at the clinic. Of course, your pup is welcome. I would love to meet her."

"And your mom?" He studied her curiously. Now her eyes seemed to twinkle with impish delight.

"Let's just consider it part of Mom's intervention. We are determined to ensure she has a very messy Christmas."

"Well, she's off to a brilliant start." He laughed as he went down the steps with a bucket in each hand. And as he walked back to his house, he felt encouraged. Maybe there was still hope for Olivia and him. That is, if Mrs. Bradshaw could ever get past her unreasonable, irrational, aggravating aversion to and general dislike of his entire family. As if that were even possible.

fifteen

AT FIRST MALCOLM and even his pup didn't seem to bother her mother, but after just two days and several puppy puddles that Olivia cleaned up quickly, she knew her mom was like a time bomb about to blow. And so Olivia planned a little meeting with her dad and grandma in the den. So far, the McEntires had been unable to locate a septic service that wasn't booked until a full week after Christmas. To help them in the duration, they'd even had a porta potty set up in their front yard. They couldn't put it in back because the company couldn't get their truck through the small gate. To help it look more festive, Cindy and Erik had decorated the little structure with a blow-up Santa who looked like he was waiting his turn. Jane did not find it amusing.

"Are we ever going to do a proper intervention?" Olivia asked her dad as soon as they gathered in his den.

"Seems like it's already begun," he said wryly.

"Yeah, the universe has dealt Jane a whammy of a hand." Lulu laughed. "I don't see how we could've done a better job."

"And your mother seems to be managing it," Dad added. "Why not just let it ride?"

"Because Mom is fuming. Sure, she's managing to contain it somehow, but I can tell she's about to explode. And to be honest, I'm getting worried about her physical health. What if she has a stroke or heart attack or something?"

Her dad's brow furrowed. "She does have elevated blood pressure."

"I'd hate to think all this could really hurt her. That would be horrible," Lulu said.

"Pastor Justin offered to help us if we do a real intervention." Dad counted on his fingers. "It's only three days until Christmas. I suppose I sort of hoped we'd get past the holiday before confronting her."

Olivia stood, pacing back and forth in front of the big-screen TV. "But what if we did a loving and honest sort of intervention, and what if Mom really got it? I mean, it's possible she could see the light. And then we could hold her hand and walk her through learning to let go of things."

"But she's been letting go," Dad persisted.

Lulu nodded. "Life has been forcing her to let go. Well, life and her wheelchair."

"But it hasn't been her choice. And from what I've read about OCD and other mental health issues, the individual has to make a choice themself. They have to engage and want to change. They need to recognize a need for help and be willing to get that help. Right now, she's more like a prisoner in her home." She held up a finger. "In fact, I've heard her say that very thing. She said she feels like a POW. And she doesn't even know what started the war."

"Good points," Lulu agreed. "I never had a counseling degree, but back at the commune I was considered the counselor."

"The commune?" Olivia studied her grandma.

"Oh, it was short-lived. I suppose your mom never mentioned it. Moonbeam was pretty small when Al and I split. She was about three by the time I realized I'd hooked up with a pot-smoking hippie who didn't believe in work. Anyway, I felt sort of lost, so I joined this free people commune in Northern California. I liked their philosophy—everyone helping everyone, getting back to nature by growing our own food, making candles and baking bread and sewing quilts . . . all that sort of thing. Supposedly there was time to breathe and contemplate and live intentionally on this commune . . . but it seemed we never really had time since there were so many chores to be done just to survive. And it eventually got too woo-woo extreme for me, and I had to take Moonbeam and get out of there." She chuckled. "But while I was still there, I got known as the counselor since I listened to everyone's problems and apparently gave good advice. And I finally advised myself to take my little girl and split."

Olivia nodded. That all made sense in a puzzling sort of way. Her mom had obviously experienced a rather interesting, perhaps frustrating, childhood. And in a weird way, hearing her grandma confessing this much gave her hope. If it was true that disorders sometimes skipped a generation, maybe she'd be more like her grandma than her mom. Or even like her dad, although she was more of a creative type and had never wanted to be an accountant.

"So, what's the next step?" Lulu asked Dad.

He rubbed his chin. "Well, I think Olivia is right. We should do this properly. I'll call Justin and see when he has time." He turned to Olivia. "Do you want to invite Malcolm and his parents to join us? I think their perspective would be good."

She nodded. "And I'm sure they'd be glad to help."

"Speaking of help." Dad stood up. "I think I hear Jane's bell ringing. I'd better check on her."

After he left, Lulu looked at Olivia. "How are you doing, honey? Your dad mentioned how you and Malcolm had been getting romantically involved. And although Malcolm is staying here, I've barely seen him. It seems all he does here is shower and sleep, and then he leaves Sadie in your care and is gone. I'd hoped to get to know him a bit. But he hasn't even remained here for a meal. Is he afraid of my cooking?" She winked.

"No. He's just super busy. First he was helping his dad with their plumbing challenges. Until their tank gets emptied, they're living like pioneer people. And then he's been helping Dr. Wheeler, who owns the vet clinic in town. I think he's testing Malcolm out, perhaps to take him on as an associate."

Lulu nodded in approval. "So, tell me . . . is it serious between you two?"

Olivia considered her answer. "To be honest, I'm not sure anymore. I mean, I really like him a lot. But you've seen how my mom treats his family."

"I know there's some kind of history there. I don't know the full story."

"The short version is that Cindy doesn't measure up to Mom's type A standards. Of course, no one does."

"Right. It really seemed she was softening up toward Cindy. But it was short-lived. When Cindy was here yesterday to explain why the little outhouse is there and how their family is still coming for Christmas, I was worried Jane was going to throw something at the poor woman."

Olivia cringed.

"After Cindy left, your mother went into a tirade over how they should've replaced their septic system ages ago. Good grief, you'd think the McEntires' sewage had flooded your parents' front yard. Your mother even threatened to call the board of health." She shrugged. "And I'll admit it does smell a little outside. But it's just temporary. And it's not like anyone is having a barbecue."

"It is pretty stinky." Olivia sighed. "It's so sad for the McEntires. Such a bind. I wish I could invite Malcolm and his family to spend Christmas with us. I mean, can you imagine trying to cook for twenty or more people with no plumbing—and that stench?"

"That'd be perfect," Lulu declared. "We will do that."

"Do what?"

"Invite them all for Christmas."

Olivia blinked. "Seriously?"

"Why not? It can be the cherry on top of Jane's little intervention sundae. And just imagine a house full of happy people gathered here. I've been in Cindy's house. This place is bigger and has a much better layout for entertaining."

"That's true." Olivia tried to imagine her mom's reaction, then decided it was better not to think about it.

"And to take the pressure off you, I'll invite them." Lulu grinned. "I'll go over there right now and start putting together a plan with Cindy. She's such a delightful person."

"Maybe you should ask them about participating in Mom's intervention while you're there," Olivia suggested, thinking she'd prefer to have that one off her shoulders too. Maybe she was cowardly, but she just wanted to preserve her relationship with her mother. And Lulu seemed skilled at ignoring conflict

. . . and thrived on acting like all was well when it was really going somewhere in a handbasket.

While Lulu went next door, Olivia went to check on her mom, discovering she'd sent Dad out for an order of Thai food.

"It just hit me," she explained to Olivia in a slightly hushed tone, "that if I ordered takeout dinner, your grandmother would not need to concoct some horrid meal." She smiled victoriously.

"That's a great idea." Olivia sat down on the sofa across from her. "How's your hip feeling? Are you staying on top of your pain management?"

"Your father just gave me a pill. I'm fine." She scowled.

"You don't sound fine."

Jane twisted a tissue in her hand, coiling it tight.

Olivia leaned forward. "You seem troubled, Mom. Are you okay?"

Jane's eyes flashed with anger. "Of course not. How could I possibly be okay?"

Olivia just nodded, waiting . . . hoping for a breakthrough.

"Good grief, can you imagine how humiliating it was to be taken by ambulance to the hospital—with bright blue hair and a clay facial mask that was cracking up?"

Olivia couldn't help but giggle. "I bet you were a sight, Mom." She sobered. "I'm sorry."

"And injuring my hip was no walk in the park either." She pointed to her wheelchair. "Then being stuck in this thing, unable to perform the simplest tasks without help."

"I don't mind helping you, Mom." Olivia knew that was only partially true. Her persnickety mother was not the easiest person in the world to assist. It seemed she never got anything quite right or good enough to satisfy her.

"And I appreciate that, Olivia. But on top of everything else, I have to endure my lunatic mother, the queen of bad taste, taking over my home and my kitchen." She glanced over her shoulder. "I'm afraid to go in there and see what a mess she's made of my beautiful kitchen."

"It's not that bad." Okay, Olivia knew that was a lie. But Mom seemed so tormented, she just had to throw her a bone.

"And now having the neighbors traipsing in and out, using my shower and my towels and who knows what else."

"Erik and Cindy can't bathe at their house, Mom. And they're using my bathroom, and I've been doing the cleanup and laundry."

"What about Malcolm?"

"He's barely here, Mom." Olivia was losing her patience. It was one thing to get her mom to open up, but it was feeling more like a dam that had been broken. How to stop the flood?

"But he's here. And no one even asked me." Jane narrowed her eyes. "And what about that dog? You might try to hide it, but I know she piddles and who knows what else on my floors when you let her run around. And my living room is starting to smell like a dog. Does she have to be in here?" She glared at the kennel carrier sitting in front of the never-used white stone-faced fireplace. The only other thing on the pristine hearth was a neat stack of birch logs tied with a blue velvet ribbon—for show, not burning.

"Sadie needs to be where I can hear her if she whines. And I haven't let her roam unsupervised since her last accident," Olivia said defensively. "And Malcolm showed me how to train her to use potty pads. We're working on it." She started to stand. "Maybe I should—"

"No, that's not the worst part, Olivia." Jane pursed her lips. "What about Malcolm? How long does he—and that dog—plan to remain in *my* house?"

Olivia took a deep breath, measuring her words. "Well, Dad said Malcolm and Sadie could stay as long as necessary. And being that the McEntires still don't have plumbing, it seemed kinder to just have one less person at their house for now. Although their family is still coming into town for Christmas."

"So I've heard." She leaned her head back, looking up at the ceiling with an exasperated expression. "Which I have to say is the most ridiculous thing ever. A houseful of people and no plumbing." She let out a sarcastic laugh.

"But they love having family there for the holidays."

"Trust me, I'm aware. But think about it, Olivia, all those people, those kids, that stupid outhouse. It's unsanitary. Really, it should be illegal. I swear they are turning into the Beverly Hillbillies over there."

Olivia laughed. "Well, this isn't exactly Beverly Hills, and the McEntires aren't enjoying their time without plumbing." She carefully considered her next sentence. "But as long as we're on the subject of the McEntires and Christmas, you should probably know that Grandma thought we should invite them to join us for Christmas." She braced herself.

Jane sat up straight, nostrils literally flaring. "*Over my dead body.*"

"Hopefully not." Olivia attempted a calm smile. "Mom, it's the neighborly thing to do. We just thought—"

"This is *my* house."

"It's Dad's house too. And I used to think it was mine, but I'm not so sure anymore. Anyway, I know Dad will agree to this idea. He really likes the McEntires. And so do I—and sharing Christmas with them would be a lot of fun. More fun than the usual formal affairs you like to host." Olivia blinked when, for the first time in her memory, the unthinkable happened. She witnessed her mother using bad language. "*Mom!*"

"I'm sorry," Jane snapped. "No, I'm not. I don't care. This is the most outrageous idea ever! I won't allow it. I'll tell your father as soon as he gets back. I swear, Olivia, there is no way on God's green earth we will invite the McEntires for Christmas."

Olivia stood, determined to remain calm or at least sound like it. "It's already a done deal. Grandma's next door right now, making a plan with Cindy. They'll share the cooking chores. Cindy is a wonderful cook." She continued to ramble about what fun they'd have with the children and playing games and singing carols . . . but her mother was fuming. If it were humanly possible, steam would probably be shooting out of her ears by now. But Olivia didn't care. It was about time her mother learned the world didn't revolve around her and her obsession with perfection.

"This is not going to happen, Olivia Elizabeth. I will put my foot down." Jane shook a fist. "I plan to tell Rob to set everyone straight as soon as he gets back. He can just uninvite the McEntires. Because we are not having them for Christmas. And that is that!"

Olivia just nodded. "Okay. Well, unless you need something, I'm going to give Sadie another lesson on her puppy pad."

Jane's response was a groan, and before she could make more protests, Olivia left to get the pup set up for a potty lesson by the back door. As she waited for Sadie to do her business, she wondered if her mom was partially right. Maybe it wasn't such a great idea to have their neighbors here after all. It wasn't as if the holidays could get any worse for the Bradshaws, but what if it spoiled the McEntire family's Christmas?

sixteen

SHORTLY AFTER Pastor Justin arrived, followed by Rob and Cindy McEntire, and finally their son Malcolm, Jane grew suspicious. Something weird was going on here. Everyone, including her mother, husband, daughter, and even that blasted little dog, were gathered in her living room. *Her* living room? That was laughable. With all the cheesy trinkets Lulu had liberally spread about, it no longer felt like her living room. Even when she'd attempted to remove the things within the reach of her wheelchair, it made little difference. In her opinion, Christmas was irredeemably wrecked.

Justin cleared his throat, folded his hands, and looked directly at her. "Jane, we have gathered here for a reason, but first I'd like to open in prayer." And then he, and the others, all bowed their heads while he prayed. Although she bowed her head, Jane knew she wasn't really praying, wasn't even listening. All she could think was that something was going on.

"Well, Jane, you may have guessed by now that this little

impromptu gathering is for your benefit." His smile looked sympathetic and a bit uneasy.

Jane nervously fingered the scarf hiding her blue hair, then shrugged.

"Because we all love you and care about your well-being, both physically and emotionally, we wanted to come together to express our concern." He glanced around the room. "You know everyone here. Do you believe that they all love you and care about you?"

She felt a hot wave of indignation rising up in her, but she wanted to conceal it. After all, this was her pastor . . . and she had her pride. Well, what was left of it. So she just mutely nodded. But she wondered, did these people truly love her? Or were they just here to torture her?

"Good." His smile looked more relaxed. "I've invited everyone here to speak openly and honestly about what concerns them. And like I just prayed, I hope we all have ears to hear . . . most of all you, Jane." He glanced at Rob. "Would you like to begin?"

Rob leaned forward in his chair, grasping his hands like he did when he was about to broach a subject she did not want to discuss. "Well, Jane, as you know, I can get frustrated over your perfectionist habits. You know the sort of things I mean. And in the past, I felt like you could hear me, and you would attempt to rein yourself in. But I've noticed that over the past, say, ten years, your obsessions have grown. So much that I'm worried for your mental health. Honey, it's almost like you torment yourself . . . as much as you torment me. And to be totally honest, it worries me. I'm not sure we—and I mean our marriage—can survive too much more of this."

Jane leaned back now, feeling as if she'd been publicly

slapped. She wanted to lash out at him and demand why he would say such a mean thing, but seeing the others all watching with wide eyes, she kept her mouth shut.

"I have to agree with Dad," Olivia began slowly. "It's hard to say this, Mom, but having some distance makes me see things more clearly. You are getting worse all the time. So much so that I don't want to come home anymore. And what makes me really sad is seeing you living in this prison of perfection that you've created. When I accidentally broke your Lladró angel, I thought you wanted to kill me. Like that object was more precious to you than I am." Olivia's eyes brimmed with tears now, making Jane almost feel guilty. And yet this all seemed so unfair. Like they were ganging up on her. Like their intent was to smear her name. But why? What had she done to deserve this inhumane treatment? Still, she said nothing.

One by one, they went around the room, sans Malcolm, who'd gotten a text on his phone that tore him away from this intimate little gathering of "friends," but that was neither here nor there to Jane as the remaining people took turns sharing their "helpful" bits and pieces, all aimed like poison darts at their cornered victim. But Jane felt herself getting angrier and angrier—so much so that their honey-coated venomous words floated over her. *Like water over a duck's back,* she thought as she closed her eyes, wishing they would all just *poof*—depart her house and leave her alone with her misery.

"Enough!" she finally shouted. "Why don't you all just crucify me like they did Jesus? You've shamed me and condemned me—why not just finish me off and put me out of my pain." And now she began to cry. Rob jumped up to put his arms around her, followed by Olivia, but she just shrugged them both off, attempting to wheel herself around, which she wasn't good at doing, but she wanted to escape to her bedroom, where she planned to lock her door until New Year's and hopefully starve herself to death.

"Oh, Jane," Rob said with a choked voice. "We don't want to hurt you, we want to help you. But if it hurts now and helps later, it'll be worth it. Can't you consider what you've heard? All that we've just confessed to you? Don't you realize we're only speaking the truth? Hoping that it'll help you to change?"

"OCD is a real condition," Olivia said. "Obsessive compulsion is very serious, Mom. And I feel pretty sure that you have it. But from what I've read, it's treatable. But you have to agree to it."

"You need professional help," Justin said in a firm but gentle tone. "I have several contacts I can share with you."

Jane locked eyes with him. "What makes you think this is my problem? What if you are all wrong? What if I'm the one who is normal and the rest of you have problems?" She pointed at Cindy. "For instance, you are a mess. Your house is a mess. For Pete's sake, you have an outhouse in your front yard! Is that normal?" She turned to Lulu. "And what about you? You bring all your trashy Christmas decorations and spread them all over my house, and I'm supposed to act like that's okay? And you, Olivia, my own daughter. You come home with Malcolm McEntire and his dog in tow—parking them in my house, and acting like that's a good idea?"

"I just wanted to be a good neighbor," Olivia said quietly.

"I think you all have been trying to drive me nutty," Jane retorted. "And you're almost succeeding."

"They just want to show you that you need help, Jane." Justin knelt down in front of her, looking her in the eye. "Everyone in this room loves you, Jane. They have all put up with your compulsions and your harsh criticisms, and they still love you. The choice will be yours, Jane. You can continue on your road to perfection, but you need to understand that your concept of perfection is very flawed. You think perfection is having the best of everything, and everyone and everything in its perfect place. But that is not God's kind of perfection. Can't you see that he made us to be flawed, he made life to have bumps and lumps, he allows hard stuff into our lives? And he does so for a reason."

"Really?" Jane challenged him. "Tell me why that is. Why would a perfect God allow so much imperfection? Why would he put up with it?"

"I believe he allows it in order to remind us that in our weakness, our brokenness, our faultiness, we need to call on him. His strength is made perfect in our weakness. And we all have a lot of weaknesses, which gives him a lot of room to show his perfection. But it's his brand of perfection—not ours. Can you see that?"

Jane realized that she wanted to see it, wanted to understand it, but felt like she was in a thick fog. "I . . . don't know."

"Do you want to see it? Do you want to understand how God's perfection is vastly different from ours? Do you want to learn to give up your standards of perfection and replace them with God's?"

She closed her eyes and considered his words, then slowly nodded. "I do want that. But to be honest, it sounds impossible. It sounds too hard." When she opened her eyes, more tears were flowing.

"But can you see that you're living in a kind of bondage, trying to create a perfect world that only hurts you and others and will eventually separate you from God and the ones you love?"

"I can sort of see that . . . through the fog," she conceded, wiping at her tears with a tissue Cindy handed to her. "But I don't know what to do about it."

"Do you trust the people in this room?" Jason asked.

She looked around, unsure that she really did trust everyone. Oh, sure, they looked sincere enough, but did they really care about her the way they claimed?

"Do you trust your husband? Your daughter? Your mother?" he persisted.

"I guess so."

"And your neighbors, who've put up with you all these years?"

She wanted to question who put up with who, but knew she was outnumbered, and so her answer was another shrug.

"Do you trust me?" he asked.

She just nodded.

"Well, right after Christmas, I want you to meet with a licensed therapist who's a close friend of me and my wife and a real expert on OCD, since she wrote her thesis on it. I already asked her to save you an appointment slot, just in case. Anyway, I'll have her give you a call to set it up."

Jane agreed to this but wondered if she would really go see this woman. Still, she felt her best chance of escaping this well-meaning albeit intrusive crowd was to agree and comply—if only for the moment. But now everyone in the room was patting her on the back, hugging her, congratulating her, and making her feel like she had just made a commitment at some evangelical rally . . . when she still questioned her sincerity and was already feeling guilty for being disingenuous.

"I'm very tired and my hip is aching," she told them, which was partly true. "I think I need a pain pill and a nap. Thank you all for coming. I'm going to be giving this a lot of thought."

Her mother began to sing "We Wish You a Merry Christmas," but instead of *merry* Lulu substituted the word *messy*, and the others, who seemed to love it, chimed right in. As Jane wheeled herself toward the bedroom, they boisterously serenaded her, and all she could think was *Get me outta here.*

In the silent security of her bedroom, with the door safely locked, she allowed herself to ponder the things that had just been said. On some level they made sense and almost rang true, but on many other levels their interference felt highly intrusive, not to mention impossible. The mere idea that she could change her ways and accept anything less than perfection when she still believed it was not only attainable but preferable . . . well, it just sounded too hard. She looked up at the framed print hanging above her cherry dresser. It was an attractive landscape of a Tuscan vineyard estate, the sort of place she'd been dreaming of visiting after Rob retired.

The bucolic scene of rich, verdant green was washed in golden sunshine—a dreamy sort of place one might see in a beautiful movie. But as lovely as the painting was, she couldn't enjoy it because it was hanging crooked on the wall. So aggravating, and it was impossible for her to reach in her current condition. And so she just sat there staring, feeling tears trickling down her cheeks and wondering if she would be stuck like this forever. "Dear God, help me," she prayed, "please, please, help me."

seventeen

DESPITE THE FACT that Malcolm was sleeping in their guest room, Olivia had barely seen him. Oh, she knew he'd been busy helping his dad and then working at the clinic. But she also knew that couldn't take all of his time. She tried not to resent how quickly he'd swooped into the house the last couple days. After returning from the clinic, he'd go upstairs and shower, then gather Sadie up and disappear. She knew he was at his parents' home, probably enjoying good food and happy company, but she still wondered if there was more going on. Was this a hint that having a relationship with her was pointless?

He was polite enough. And he really seemed to appreciate the time she was spending with Sadie. In fact, she had fallen in love with Sadie and secretly wished she could keep the little dog. So when he informed her that his mother had offered to take over puppy-sitting—just two days before Christmas—she felt slighted and hurt. Oh, sure, it was childish. Sadie wasn't hers. And obviously, Malcolm wasn't either. But the thought of losing him—if she'd ever had him—hurt more than she cared to admit. But consequently, she wasn't in what anyone would describe as a cheery state of mind as she cleaned the kitchen and loaded the dishwasher that evening.

"Are you slamming things around in here for a reason?" Lulu asked from behind her.

"Sorry, was I too noisy?" Olivia rinsed her hands, wiping them on a Santa towel.

"Your mother asked me to check. And she wants tea." Lulu filled the kettle.

"Is she in any better spirits?" Olivia wasn't sure she really cared but wanted to sound like a good daughter.

"She's been very quiet all afternoon and evening."

"But she came out of her room?"

"Yes. She refuses to use her walker." Lulu frowned. "That worries me a little. Rob said she's supposed to move about some to help the hip heal."

Olivia shrugged. "Well, we can't really force her."

"True enough." Lulu peered closely at Olivia. "Are you okay? You don't look well to me. I can make you an herbal tea that might perk you up."

"No, thanks." Olivia felt herself cracking at this tiny show of pity. "I guess I'm just sad."

"About Malcolm?"

"About everything. I mean, Mom is a real piece of work, and . . ."

"But this isn't really about your mother, is it?"

Olivia shrugged. "Well, partly." She bit her lip.

"You think your mother has scared off Malcolm."

Olivia grimaced. Was she that obvious?

"And it's a legitimate worry."

"Yeah, I know. But there's not much I can do about it. I

mean, I thought maybe our intervention would help, but she seems more stuck than ever. Oh, she's quieter, but she's just so stubborn."

"Might take time." Lulu measured out loose tea leaves, then put them in the pot. "Old age has taught me to be patient."

"Something to look forward to . . . when I'm an old spinster lady with a lot of cats to keep me company, since I'm pretty sure Mom will scare off any guy who's not an uptight perfectionist like her, and thanks, but no thanks."

Lulu laughed as the teakettle whistled. "Do you want to hear what I think?"

"Of course." Olivia watched as her grandmother poured steaming water into the teapot.

"I think that Malcolm still likes you—a lot more than you realize." She set the kettle back on the stove and turned to face Olivia. "I've watched him looking at you, Livvie, when you're not paying attention. I've seen the look in his eyes."

"Seriously?" Olivia felt hopeful for a couple seconds, then let out a defeated sigh. "You're probably imagining things, but even if you're right, it doesn't matter. Malcolm knows how much Mom detests his family. He can see we are not a match made in heaven." She attempted a sardonic laugh, but it sounded more like a hiccup. "And after my mother ruins his family's Christmas, which is sure to happen when they come here to celebrate . . . well, that should put a permanent kibosh on the whole thing."

"Your mother has threatened to stay in her room the whole time Malcolm's family is here, so maybe it won't matter."

"And it won't seem weird, not to mention inhospitable, for her to hide out?"

"Oh, I don't know. We can always blame her isolation on

her injury, say she's in too much pain to make an appearance." Lulu set a strainer on one of Mom's favorite teacups, slowly filling it. "It's okay to let some things go."

"I am letting some things go," Olivia pointed out. "Mainly any hopes of having a lasting relationship with Malcolm. Grandma, I know he's avoiding me. And I don't blame him a bit. I think it's time for me to move on."

"Time will tell." Lulu nodded with a sage expression. "And now I need to take your mother her tea." She winked. "I was tempted to doctor it up with something to make her relax more, but I don't want to cause a reaction with her pain meds." She chuckled as she left the kitchen.

Olivia stood in front of the kitchen window, gazing out with longing toward the McEntires' house, where their windows seemed to glow with a cheerful golden light and she could imagine music and laughter. She remembered spending time there as a child, wishing she was part of their relaxed, boisterous, fun-loving family rather than her own family. But right now, she felt separated from them, like that pathetic proverbial kid with her nose pressed to the toy store window, wishing. But she knew that even if Malcolm truly loved her—like she feared she loved him—it would be too challenging. Really, they were not so different from the Montagues and Capulets . . . just an aged-up version of *Romeo and Juliet*. But taking poison felt just a bit too extreme, even for a broken—or breaking—heart. She closed the window blinds and turned away.

* * *

As he sanded the primitive-looking carved statuette of Joseph, a wave of sadness washed over Malcolm. "Wow . . ." He sighed, set down the carving, and turned to his dad, who'd been helping him on this little project. "I don't know . . ."

"Don't know what?" Erik looked confused. "Don't get discouraged. We're almost done. Those pieces are almost ready to be sealed, and I gotta say, they're really good, son. I didn't know you had a hidden artistic side."

Malcolm picked up the Joseph figurine and held it in front of his dad. "I was just thinking about the real Joseph. You know, Jesus's stepfather."

"Uh-huh?" Erik poured more oil onto the cloth he was using to seal the other pieces of the nativity set that Malcolm had been working on for the past several days. The idea had come after Olivia had told him about the childhood set her mother had gotten rid of. He'd hoped to surprise her for Christmas, but work in the city and here at home had waylaid him a little. Fortunately, his dad, a good woodworker, was helping now. "So, tell me, son, what is it you were thinking about Joseph?"

"Well, I know it must've been hard for him." Malcolm studied the figure that he'd carved, more symbolic than realistic, although it was attractive in a rustic sort of way. And when all the pieces were put together, it wouldn't take a genius to figure out what they represented.

"Right," Erik agreed. "To become a father to the Son of God . . . those are pretty big sandals to fill."

Malcolm smiled. "For sure, but that's not exactly what I was thinking. I was thinking about him seeing all the obstacles he had to face if he married Mary. I mean, think about it, it must've been overwhelming. Don't you think?"

"So, bringing this home, Malcolm, are you thinking of the obstacles with Olivia's family? Mainly her mother?"

Malcolm nodded solemnly. "I realize it's nothing like what

Joseph faced, but at least God gave him a dream to confirm it was the right thing to do."

"Ya think God'll give you a dream?" Erik had a slight teasing edge to his voice. "But I don't mean to make light of this. I realize that Jane Bradshaw is a lot to deal with. Believe me, I know. But I also know that Rob is a good man. And Olivia is a great gal. I mean, we've known her forever, and I still remember her coming over here, playing with you kids like she was part of the family. And I know for a fact she loves her parents, but there were times she wanted to be part of this family."

Malcolm considered this. He'd been enough older than Olivia not to have noticed these things. Mostly she'd just been the neighbor kid who liked to hang with his younger sisters. Nice enough, but nothing to get his attention . . . until they'd met again as adults.

"And I really think that under Jane's veneer of perfection, which by the way seems a little crackled and peeling of late, kinda like that cabinet I just refinished for your mom . . . anyway, there's a good woman who doesn't want to be like that underneath."

Malcolm had heard about the so-called intervention from his mother. Of course, she'd given it a positive spin, but he was not convinced.

"But, Dad," he said, "Mrs. Bradshaw hates our family. How could I possibly make a serious go of it with her daughter?"

"*Hate* is a strong word." Erik picked up a wise man figure and rubbed oil into it. "I think she just doesn't understand us. Something shifted in her somewhere . . . maybe we'll never fully understand it . . . but I believe that God made her, just as surely as you made these statues, and God has a plan for her. And for all we know, you—and our family—could be a part of that. And I'll tell you something else, I feel that Rob is one of my best friends, and I'm pretty sure he feels the same—even if he hides it from Jane. So I am personally not willing to give up on them. Any of them." He picked up the Mary figure now, gazing at her. "And one more thing, I would be proud to call Olivia a daughter, and I know she would fit into our family perfectly."

Malcolm felt slightly choked up at this unexpected speech. Dad wasn't usually a real verbal sort of guy, and what he'd just said was both amazing and affirming. With the Joseph figure still in his hand, he hugged him.

"Thanks, Dad, I needed that."

"Me too," Erik said. "I wanted to say something but didn't really know how." He slapped Malcolm on the back. "For what it's worth, you have my blessing."

Malcolm thanked him again, then continued sanding a rough edge off the Joseph figure. He knew these pieces were pretty rustic but thought to himself that maybe that was fitting. Wasn't it pretty rustic at that first Christmas? Hopefully Olivia would appreciate that, because he knew for a fact her mother wouldn't.

eighteen

ON THE MORNING of Christmas Eve, Olivia got up early in hopes of catching Malcolm before he disappeared, and, seeing that the bathroom sink was dry with no signs of use, she suspected Malcolm was still sleeping in the guest room. So she tiptoed downstairs and set to making coffee, keeping her ear trained on the stairs for Malcolm's footsteps. At the very least she hoped to exchange a good morning greeting . . . and perhaps gauge his response toward her—would it be warm or cool?

She was just leaving the kitchen with her mug of coffee when Malcolm came very quietly down the stairs, carrying Sadie's doggy crate. Olivia smiled at him and held up her steaming mug. "I just made a fresh pot if you're interested."

"I'd love some." He beamed at her in a way that gave her hope.

"Follow me," she whispered, leading him to the kitchen and filling a mug. She knew he took his coffee black. "Do you have time to sit?" she asked quietly, gesturing toward Dad's den, knowing conversation in there wouldn't disturb the others still sleeping. Malcolm nodded and followed her.

"I feel like I've barely seen you the whole time you've been here," she said as she sat in her dad's favorite chair. "To be honest, I was starting to feel like you were avoiding me."

He set Sadie's crate on the floor and sat on the sofa with a thoughtful expression. "No, I wasn't avoiding you. Not at all. I was just trying not to aggravate your mother. You know how that can be." He opened Sadie's crate, taking the pup into his lap. "And I planned to keep her at my parents' house today while I'm, uh, working over there."

"If you're busy, you can leave her with me. I love having her around."

"You really do seem to like her. But I sort of overheard your mom talking to your dad when I came in last night. Kind of complaining about Sadie."

"Mom complains about everything," she said. "You just have to learn to ignore her."

"So the intervention plan didn't really work?"

"It's hard to say. I mean, it seems like she's thinking about it. But she's so miserable with the pain in her hip and her blue hair and my grandma here and all. Well, it's a lot. I almost feel sorry for her." She grinned. "*Almost*. But, really, I don't mind having Sadie here with me, especially if you're busy helping your dad. Sadie's good company." She moved from the chair to the couch, stroking Sadie's soft coat. "She makes me happy."

Malcolm beamed at her. "I love that about you, Olivia."

Olivia felt some consolation. Maybe nothing had changed between them after all. Still, she wanted to reassure him.

"Believe me, I know my mom is extremely difficult. And to be honest, I don't know if that'll ever change. Pastor Justin's suggestion for a therapist makes so much sense, if we can get her to agree to it, and even if she does . . ." She shrugged. "You know what they say about leading a horse to water."

"I know."

"But I've been learning something during my stay here."

"What's that?"

"I'm seeing that I can separate myself from her, you know, like I can emotionally step back. I don't have to feel responsible for her bad behavior. We are totally different people. I am her daughter, and I'll always love her, but I don't have to let her control my thinking or my life. As you know, she's always been a control freak. But more than ever, I'm aware that I am not her. She might want me to be, but I'm not. I think spending all this time stuck taking care of her and seeing all her weird obsessions, well, it's sort of been therapeutic for me. Does that make sense?" She studied him, somewhat surprised by her own confession because it was the first time she'd said this out loud. But she believed it.

Malcolm nodded with what looked like relief. "That's so good to hear, Olivia. Thanks for telling me that. I can see how that would happen while you've been around her so much lately."

"Yeah, instead of running away and feeling guilty like I usually do, it's like I've been thrown into the fire with her, so to speak, and it's not comfortable, but it's been a great life lesson." She sipped her coffee. "So, how are things at your parents' house? Are you resolving your plumbing problems?"

"No, that's not what I've been working on with him. That can't be resolved until they get their septic tank emptied. Although Dad found a guy over in the valley who might be willing to come in a few days. Not before Christmas, though, and it will be expensive."

"I'm glad your family is being forced to come here to celebrate. I just hope my Grinchy mom doesn't ruin it for everyone."

"Are you kidding?" He laughed. "You know my family, Livvie. They will be loud and crazy, and I'm pretty sure your mom will be drowned out by their exuberance."

"That's perfect."

"Good morning, kiddos." Dad came into the den, still wearing his bathrobe and slippers. "Thought I heard voices in here."

"Did we disturb you?" Malcolm stood.

"Nah, I was already up. But not before you early birds." He opened the blinds to a steely gray sky. "Looks like weather on the way. The forecast is snow in the mountains, but looks like it might hit the foothills too. Wouldn't it be great to have a white Christmas?"

"Oh, I hope so." Olivia pointed to her mug. "I made coffee. Want me to get you a cup?"

"Thanks, honey." Dad sat in his chair and sighed happily. "It's so great having family around. I've sure missed that. It'll be lonely when you kids go back to the city."

As Olivia went for her dad's coffee, she could still hear him and Malcolm talking. Taking her time, she listened as Malcolm explained about his work with Doc Wheeler this past week, and how it might become an opportunity for him to move back home.

"I didn't realize how much I've missed small-town living. Can't beat the commute to the clinic. Can you believe it only takes me about three minutes to get there?"

"I know what you mean. Sometimes, if the weather is good, I walk to work," Dad said.

Listening to the two men visiting congenially felt so good,

like this was what was meant to be, and she longed for it to be permanent. Was that even possible? But hearing Mom's bell ringing, she knew it was time to go assist her, and so she hurriedly took Dad his coffee and then excused herself. Today would be a long day with Mom's grim attitude toward the houseful of guests expected this evening. Olivia knew it would take more patience, prayer, and emotional distancing to get through it.

* * *

After a very trying morning of attempting to pacify her agitated mother while Grandma busily prepared things in the kitchen for the evening festivities, Olivia was ready to throw in the towel when Cindy showed up with two large shopping bags. Assuming she was bringing food and was here to assist Grandma, Olivia led her toward the kitchen.

"Hi there," Lulu called out above the cheery Christmas music. "Are you here to help?"

"Yes, but I was hoping to visit with Jane first." Cindy paused to set the bag on a barstool, then extracted a pink box from on top. "I have something for Jane for Christmas. But I wanted her to have it early."

"Mom's in her room." Olivia lowered her voice. "She's kind of sulking."

"She's definitely in a foul mood today." Lulu set a mixing bowl in the sink. "Doing a great imitation of Ebenezer Scrooge."

"Maybe this will cheer her up." Cindy smiled. "Come on and see."

"Let me get this cake in the oven first," Lulu said.

Curious and hoping the contents of that box really would

lift Mom's spirits, Olivia led the way. Hopefully it didn't contain something from the bakery since they used pink boxes too. Mom had just been complaining about being sick of sweets and predicting they'd all gain an extra ten pounds before the holidays were over. And naturally, she wanted the holidays and all the trappings and trimmings gone as soon as possible.

Olivia knocked three times like her mother had instructed, then cautiously opened the door. "Mom, there's someone here to see you."

"Tell them I'm not seeing anyone today," Jane growled from her wheelchair, which was still facing away.

"Cindy has something for you," Olivia pressed on. "Early Christmas presents."

"Tell her I'm not interested," Jane snapped. "As far as I'm concerned, Christmas is canceled this year."

"Oh, Jane," Cindy said gently. "I'm sure it must feel like that to you. Goodness, you've had such a hard go of it. But I hope you won't give up."

Jane spun her chair around to face them. She saw the gifts in Cindy's hand, but her expression was hard to read. She was probably trying to seem polite, but underneath that fake veneer she appeared to be seething.

Cindy seemed oblivious or just adept at ignoring bad manners as she sat on the chair by Jane.

"You know my middle daughter, Ruby? Well, she's a licensed hairdresser and works at a Seattle salon. So, several days ago, I asked her to hunt something down for me." She opened the pink box and removed a platinum wig, holding it up in front of Jane. It was cut in a bob that looked like an exact replica of Jane's hair—before it turned Smurf blue.

Jane blinked in astonishment. "What . . . how did you . . . I don't understand." But she wheeled her chair closer, reaching out to touch the hair. "It feels real."

"It is real." Cindy beamed at her. "I had Rob text me some photos of you that I texted to Ruby, and she managed to find this for you." She stood up. "Should we try it on?"

Jane simply nodded, waiting as Cindy fiddled with the wig. "Of course, it would probably be better if your hair was shorter or in a wig cap."

Olivia, feeling a mixture of disbelief and gratitude, held up the hand mirror for her mother. "Oh, Mom, it really looks like you."

Jane was still trying to tuck stubborn strands of damaged blue hair out of sight, but she seemed pleased. "It really does resemble my old hair," she said quietly. "Impressive." She looked up at Cindy. "I don't know what to say."

"Isn't it just perfect?" Cindy looked exuberant. "I couldn't believe it when I saw it. It looked just like you."

"Let me pay you for it—"

"No, Jane. This is a gift. Just receive it as a gift. Please."

Jane pursed her lips, then slowly nodded. "Thank you." She was still fiddling with her blue hair. "If I had some scissors, I'd just hack this horrible blue mop off."

"Maybe I can help you with that. You know, I cut Erik's hair and all the kids' hair until they got too old and wouldn't let me. I'm fairly handy with the scissors."

Jane commanded Olivia to go to her bathroom, specifying exactly which drawer to find scissors in. As Olivia fetched them, she could hear her grandmother coming into the bedroom and gushing over the wig. When she returned, she saw that Lulu was carrying a brightly colored Christmas gift bag.

"Isn't it perfect?" Olivia said as she handed Cindy the scissors and a towel and set down a wastebasket to catch the hair.

"Oh, Cindy." Lulu patted her back. "You truly are a wonder." She held up the bag. "As long as we're celebrating Christmas early, I wanted to give you this, Jane." She set the bag in Jane's lap. "I thought you might wear it tonight."

Jane's brow creased slightly, but she didn't say anything as she slowly opened the bag. Preparing for some weird item of clothing that her mother would hate, Olivia actually held her breath as red tissue paper was removed to reveal what looked like some kind of silky garment. Jane looked surprised as she extracted it. In shades of blues, greens, and a bit of silver and gray, it was a sophisticated paisley print that reminded Olivia of some of her mother's favorite scarves.

"Do you remember hostess gowns?" Lulu asked. "From the seventies? I remember seeing them in movies, but I never had one myself. Elegant ladies would use them for entertaining, and I hear they're making a comeback. At least that's what the woman at Boho Girl Boutique told me. It's something to wear if you're hosting a fancy cocktail party. Anyway, it's not really my style, but something about it reminded me of you. And if you don't like it, I will not be the least bit offended. The woman assured me you can exchange it for something else."

"Let's get a good look at it." Olivia lifted the garment from her astonished mother's lap, unfurling it and holding it up. "Oh, Mom, it's absolutely gorgeous. Look how the full skirt just flows."

"And since it's loose, it can slip right over your head and drape over your legs, so you won't have to put on these pants you've been complaining about." Lulu pointed to the detested warm-up pants.

Jane mutely nodded as she fingered the silky fabric.

"And those colors have always looked beautiful on you." Olivia held the gown up to Jane, hanging it on her shoulders as if she were dressing a paper doll. She gave her the hand mirror again. "You look quite regal."

"Queen Jane." Lulu did a mock bow.

Jane looked slightly sheepish as she gazed up at Lulu, and, unless Olivia was imagining it, her mother's eyes were getting misty. "I really don't know what to say." She turned to Cindy. "And to you too. I'm just so—so overwhelmed."

"Why don't you just tell them both thanks, Mom," Olivia urged.

Jane slowly shook her head, her eyes a mixture of wonder and confusion as she quietly thanked all three of them. "Really," she finally said. "Your kindness . . . so undeserved . . . well, it's just overwhelming." Now her tears began to flow.

Olivia handed her a tissue, and Cindy held up the scissors. "Now, if you're certain you want to do this, I'll give you a haircut to make your wig fit better." She draped the towel around Jane's shoulders.

"Maybe you'll look like a punk rocker when she's done," Olivia teased, hoping to coax a smile from her mom. But Jane just looked down at her lap, as if she really was thinking about all this. And that was probably good.

"Well, I've got work to do," Lulu said crisply.

"I'll help you," Olivia told her. And as she trailed her grandmother to the kitchen, she felt like skipping and singing. Maybe Christmas wouldn't be such a disaster after all.

nineteen

FOR A MOMENT, Rob thought he'd walked into the wrong house. For starters, some of Lulu's wild-looking Christmas decorations were missing. Not all, but some of the most obnoxious ones had been removed. But what really took him by surprise was seeing what looked like Jane—the old Jane—standing in the foyer and holding to the stair newel post. She had her old hair back and was wearing an attractive gown the color of sapphires and emeralds.

"Jane?" Keeping his eyes fixed on her, and hoping this wasn't a dream, he peeled off his snow-flecked coat, hanging it on the hall tree, and went to her. As he embraced her, he noticed her wheelchair parked behind her, and Lulu and Olivia lurking in the shadows. "Is this really you?" He peered into her face. "You look beautiful."

"I know I'm not supposed to put weight on my bad hip yet, but I just wanted to stand to greet you."

He kissed her, then chuckled. "I thought I was hallucinating for a moment. It's so good to see you like this. How did you get your hair back to normal?"

She explained about Cindy's hairdresser daughter procuring a wig and how her dress was a gift from Lulu. "And thanks to Olivia's help, some of the decorations have been toned down." She glanced at her mother.

"Looks much better," Lulu admitted. "I guess I did get carried away at the dollar store."

Olivia wheeled the chair closer to Jane. "You shouldn't overdo it, Mom."

"I'll help with that," Rob offered.

"Thanks." Olivia smiled, then glanced at something on her phone. "I have an appointment in a few minutes, so I guess I better get going."

For the first time in days Rob thought his daughter appeared sincerely happy. He suspected the relationship between her and Malcolm was steadily warming, but he didn't want to upset Jane by mentioning it. It was one thing for his wife to be in good spirits and feeling more like herself, even with hosting all the McEntires tonight for Christmas Eve, but it was something else for her to entertain thoughts of having one of their clan becoming a permanent member of the Bradshaw family. *Baby steps*, he thought as he helped ease Jane into the chair.

"And it's time for me to go help Cindy," Lulu said as she tugged on a puffy parka. "Wait'll you see all the appetizers she and her girls have whipped up. We will be feasting like kings tonight."

"Making me hungry." Rob pushed Jane's wheelchair into the living room, pausing by her favorite armchair.

"I'm feeling festive," Rob said as he helped Jane into the chair. "And you sure do look festive."

"Well, this is Christmas Eve," she said as she smoothed her skirt.

"So how about we start celebrating with some eggnog?" he offered.

"Your special recipe?" Her eyes twinkled.

"Of course." He grinned. "I got all the ingredients the other day. Thought we could use some extra help stirring up our Christmas cheer this year." He stopped himself from reminding her of their houseful of guests later this evening.

But as he mixed their eggnogs, he had it in mind and was perhaps a bit more generous with the brandy. And since Jane was no longer taking pain meds, he didn't think it would hurt. He put their drinks on a Christmas tray, added some napkins and a plate of delicious-looking cookies, then carried it out to her and set it on the coffee table.

"Very nice." She nodded her approval.

He handed her a mug, then made a toast. "Here's to a wonderful holiday, unlike anything we've ever had before."

Her forehead creased slightly. "No doubt."

He sat in the chair next to her as they sipped their drinks. "I'm so proud of you, Jane."

"Proud of me?" Her brows arched.

"The way you're handling things. I know this Christmas hasn't been easy for you." And, he thought, it could get even harder if Olivia and Malcolm moved in the direction he suspected they were headed. Not that he planned to mention that.

She sighed and looked around, frowning slightly, probably disapproving of Lulu's bright touches still sprinkled about. "You're right. So much this year has been out of control and extremely difficult. I have to admit I really did want to cancel Christmas."

"Yes, but look at you. Out here being cheerful." He beamed at her. "And beautiful. Honestly, sweetie, I'm very impressed."

"I'm trying." Her smile looked weak but genuine.

Rob glanced at the flameless fireplace, white and pristine and cold.

"I know what you're thinking," Jane said quietly.

"It's Christmas, Jane. Remember when we used to have real wood fires in that?"

"Back when it was brick and ugly . . . before I got it refaced with that pretty white stone," she said with a grim expression. "You really want to blacken it now?"

He barely nodded. "But it's okay. Never mind."

She shrugged and took another sip of her drink. "Go ahead."

He blinked. "Seriously?"

"That's what it's for. Light it."

He got up eagerly, pointing to her pretty stack of birch logs. "And those?"

"Why not." Her tone sounded flat but when he turned to look at her, she gave him a lopsided smile. "I can always get more."

"Alrighty." He untied the ribbon and neatly stacked the logs in the fireplace, shoving in some twisted pieces of today's newspaper here and there. "The wood's certainly well dried," he said as he pulled out a long wooden matchstick from the sleek lacquered box. These weren't only for show, since Jane occasionally used a match to light a candle. The flame quickly flared up around the logs and paper, and he stood back to admire it.

Smoke began to billow out.

"The flue!" Jane yelled.

"Oh no!" Rob leaped into action.

"Don't burn yourself," she cried as he reached in and pulled the metal handle.

Standing up and flailing his arms like fan blades in an attempt to redirect the smoke, he knew it was useless. He turned to Jane with a sheepish smile. “Sorry about that.”

Her cheerful demeanor was cloudy now, but she held out her mug with an impish smile. “Another eggnog might help.”

This time, he held back a bit on the brandy. No point in getting snookered before the guests arrived. By the time he got back, the fire was crackling nicely.

“Very cozy,” he said as he set their refreshed drinks down. “I could light the candles too,” he suggested carefully. He knew that Jane had her own rules about candles. Some were for lighting and some were for show. “If you wanted?”

She nodded. “Go for it.”

“Okay.” But as Rob lifted the hurricane glass to light the arrangement of creamy white candles, he wasn’t sure whether to be happy or concerned. He didn’t want to push her too far. But to emphasize the golden glow of the candles, he used the dimmer to turn down the chandelier. “How’s that?”

“Better. Mom’s dollar store–decorations seem a little less gaudy in this light.” Jane actually smiled. “In fact, it’s beautiful.”

“It is.” He sat down and turned toward her. “Just like you.” And it was true, she really did look beautiful in this light. And with a sweet smile too. It reminded him of how she used to be before she turned into such a control freak. And as they sat there, enjoying the ambiance of fire and candlelight and quiet Christmas music, he tried to remember what had started her on this path in the first place. Oh, he knew it was partly a reaction to her unconventional messy childhood. And he’d always wondered if it was related to the babies she’d lost when Olivia was too small to understand, and the consequent decision to quit trying to increase their family.

And maybe it wasn't that important for him to know all the reasons, but to simply support and encourage her to return to a healthier state.

"When will the McEntires come?" she asked.

"Oh, didn't I tell you they were going to the five o'clock candlelight service before coming here? I told everyone we'd pass on it this year since it's icy out there, and with your hip and all."

"I appreciate that."

"And it sounded like your mother was going to go with them. I'm not sure about Olivia."

"Nice to have a few hours before chaos erupts." She leaned back and gazed at the mantle clock. "It's barely four o'clock and already dusky outside."

"Some peace and quiet to ourselves." He wasn't sure how long Olivia would be gone, but he suspected she was with Malcolm. "You know, Jane, I was doing some thinking earlier today . . . about, you know, some of the issues we talked to you about the other day with Pastor Justin."

"My obsessive compulsions." She scowled. "Are you about to lecture me on how I need to meet with Justin's therapist friend too?"

"No, not at all. I didn't mean to go there," he said quickly. "Actually, it all got me thinking about the first Christmas."

"The first Christmas? You mean when we first got married?"

"No, I mean the one we celebrate, when Jesus was born." He smiled. "And since we can't make it to the candlelight service . . ." He waved to the candles. "Maybe we can sort of have one of our own."

"Oh?" She studied him. "Are you going to read the nativity

story from the Bible like you used to do for Olivia when she was young?"

"Not exactly." He considered his words. "And I'm no preacher, but I got to thinking about heaven."

"Heaven?" She leaned forward with worried eyes. "Oh, Rob, please, don't tell me you're thinking about death. Are you sick?"

"No, no." He waved a hand in dismissal. "I was thinking about Jesus, the Son of God, and what he had to give up in heaven to come to earth. Now, I'm no expert, but from what I've read and heard, heaven must be amazingly spectacular and beautiful. I personally think earth is incredibly beautiful. The parts humans haven't damaged, anyway. Which makes me think of something else. You know, God created a perfect world with mountains and oceans and flowers and trees and animals and . . . well, you get the picture. Anyway, I think most people agree that humanity has managed to mess a lot of that up. Think about it. Between war and greed and thoughtlessness, there are places on earth that are pretty sad and disgusting and messy, all thanks to humanity. I wonder how that makes God feel. But that's not my main point." He chuckled. "Just a little rabbit trail I went down recently."

"But you make a good point. God is a perfectionist." Jane seemed vindicated.

"Yes, but his idea of perfection is a whole lot different from ours."

"I suppose." She leaned back, listening.

"Anyway, back to Jesus. So, he's there in this amazing place that's unspoiled by humanity's greed or stupidity. No pollution, no wars, no hatred. And God decides to send him to earth. So where does God send him? Not to a palace that wouldn't even begin to match the beauty of heaven. Not even to a nice home. No, God sends Jesus down to a shelter for animals. Whether it was a barn or a cave or a stable is for historians to argue over, but it was where they kept donkeys and cows and oxen. And it was winter. Can you imagine what it smelled like? Or what it looked like? Dirt and straw and animal feces all around."

Jane wrinkled her nose. "Sounds pretty disgusting."

"And messy."

She merely nodded.

"So, the Son of God is born in the midst of messiness. And for some reason God felt that was the perfect place for him. And Jesus, who was perfect, came into a world that was one great big mess, in every way imaginable. And yet that was exactly what God wanted. It was perfect. And it was perfect that Jesus lived among messy, he walked alongside messy, and he dwelled right next door to messy."

He paused in his unexpected sermonette to see if Jane was following his reasoning, and she seemed fully focused. So he continued. "Just think about the kinds of people Jesus dined with, visited in their homes. Messy people with messy lives. He was perfect, but he reached out to poor smelly fishermen, he befriended shunned prostitutes, he invited despised tax collectors to dinner. He even touched lepers who were so messy and afflicted and smelly that no one wanted to be anywhere near them. Perfect meets messy. With no judgment. No condemnation. Nothing but kindness and grace from the Son of God as he engages with messy people and messy lives. Our perfect Savior remained right in their midst, engaging, befriending, helping, healing, redeeming."

He sighed and took a slow sip of eggnog. "That's a lot to wrap your head around."

She just nodded with a thoughtful expression.

And then they both just sat there in the peaceful space, absorbing the sights, smells, sounds of Christmas . . . and Rob felt hopeful.

twenty

THE COFFEE SHOP was busier than Malcolm had expected, as he'd thought other people would be busily getting ready for Christmas. But maybe that was for the older generation, like his parents, since most of the customers in here appeared to be more of his age group. He wondered if they all lived here in town or were visiting their folks for the holidays. And he wondered if he could really fit back into small-town culture like he'd just assured Doc Wheeler he was ready to do.

Admittedly, his reentry back into the home front would be much smoother with the right woman by his side. But was the right woman ready for that? And was Olivia really the right woman? Most of the time he believed she was, he wanted her to be, but sometimes her uptight mother was unsettling. And what if Olivia wasn't interested in living in her hometown? After all, she had her life in the city. And sometimes she seemed perfectly happy there. Maybe he was moving too fast. Maybe giving up the security of his demanding job at the city clinic was like jumping from the frying pan into the fire.

After all, Doc Wheeler's goal was retirement. What if Malcolm wasn't ready to carry the workload that came with running his own practice?

But he shoved all those troublesome thoughts aside as Olivia walked in the door. As usual, she looked fresh and pretty with her auburn hair partly tucked under a dark knitted cap dusted with snow, the rest curling around her cold flushed cheeks. Her eyes lit up when she spotted him. He pointed to the coffee mug next to him, and she broke into a grateful smile to see he'd already ordered for her. She peeled off her parka and sat down with what sounded like a happy sigh.

"Having a good day?" he asked.

"Surprisingly." She told him about her mom's early Christmas gifts and how she'd seemed genuinely changed or at least changing. "It felt nothing short of miraculous. Especially since she'd been threatening to lock herself in her room until Christmas was over. And considering her bad attitude, I don't think anyone would've minded. Well, other than Dad. It's so sweet. I mean, I can tell he really loves her despite, well, everything." She paused to pick up her latte, smiling at the heart cut into the foam, then took a sip.

"That's good to hear. Amazing, really. Do you think that intervention had anything to do with it?"

"Maybe partly. But I honestly think it was your mom's kindness with the wig and haircut and everything. And Grandma's help too. It's like they were speaking her love language. They got through to her, made her feel understood." She shrugged. "Of course, it might all wear off. No telling with my mom. But it did feel like progress. Just the same, I plan to urge her to see Pastor Justin's counselor friend after the new year."

"Couldn't hurt. Speaking of Pastor Justin, do you want to

go to the early candlelight service with me? That's what my family is doing. It starts in about forty minutes."

She nodded eagerly. "I'd love to. Thanks." She glanced around. "Where's Sadie? I thought you might have her with you."

"It's pretty cold out for her. I took her for a little walk right before I came here. And she loved the snow. You should've seen her biting at it, rolling in it. I wish I'd taken a video. But by the time we got home, she was so worn out. So I just dried her off, fed her, and put her in her crate for a long winter nap."

"Oh, I wish I'd seen her in the snow. She's such a sweetie. I missed her today."

"You really do like her, don't you?"

"Of course. I love her. She's a darling." Olivia looked like she wanted to say something more, but she suddenly seemed a bit shy as she looked down, fiddling with her napkin. Then she looked up, locking eyes with him. "You said you wanted to meet me here for a special reason . . . and, okay, I'm dying of curiosity. What's up?"

"Two special reasons." He told her about Doc Wheeler's job offer.

"That's wonderful, Malcolm! Although I'm not the least bit surprised. Of course, he wants you. Why wouldn't he? But congratulations. That's great. I mean, I assume you accepted it?"

He nodded. "I said yes, but to be honest, I'm still playing the pros and cons in my head. But the pros seem to be way ahead."

"Good for you." She bit her lower lip then smiled. "I'm really happy for you."

For a long moment, they both just sat there sipping their

coffee, while all around them were voices and laughter and jazzy Christmas music . . . until finally Olivia spoke.

"You said *two* reasons. What's the other?"

He reached for the shopping bag sitting on the floor next to him and held it up. "This isn't really from Emilia's," he explained. "I just begged a bag from my mom. You know how she saves everything." He laughed. "Anyway, it's something I, uh, I made for you. I didn't want it to wait for Christmas. Because, well, I thought you could use it beforehand. Maybe." He handed it to her.

"It's heavy." She tested the twine handles. "Do I get to open it now?"

"Of course." He watched as she pulled out the sturdy cardboard box, also scavenged from his mom, but just right for the nativity set. He held his breath as she lifted the lid, pulled back some white tissue paper, and removed a carved piece. A shepherd.

"Oh, Malcolm." She looked at him with wide eyes. "Seriously? You made this?"

He nodded, smiling uncontrollably. "It's what I've been doing over at my parents' house. Dad helped me with a few things. But I mostly made it. I remember you telling me about the plastic set you had, and how your mom got rid of it. So I thought you needed a new one."

She was eagerly removing more pieces, setting them on the bistro table one by one. "I can't believe you made these. So creative."

"Well, the style is kind of rustic. But that's on purpose. I thought it was fitting."

"It's absolutely perfect, Malcolm. I totally love it. Thank you so much." She got up from her chair to hug him, kissing him solidly on the cheek. "I really love, love, love it." And now she grabbed his chin and planted a big kiss right on his lips. "Thank you." She stepped back, looking slightly embarrassed to have done that in public. "I hope that was okay."

He grinned. "It was better than okay."

A few curious onlookers approached their table to admire the nativity set, asking where they'd gotten it, and Olivia proudly explained Malcolm had made it. But when they asked if they could order more sets, he explained this one was one of a kind.

"A labor of love," he told a woman balancing a toddler on her hip.

The woman turned to Olivia. "You're one lucky girl."

"I know." Olivia beamed at Malcolm.

By the time Olivia had admired every piece in the set and packed them neatly away and they'd finished their coffees, it was time to head over to church. He carried her shopping bag in one hand, and in the other hand he held onto hers. And as they walked the short distance through town, he could imagine a small-town life like this . . . with a woman like this. And with the glowing streetlamps and strings of Christmas lights reflected on the shiny surface of snow, he felt this evening was truly magical. With Olivia by his side and the hope of more sweet kisses to come, well, despite their slightly bumpy start, this was promising to be a very good Christmas.

twenty-one

THEIR CHRISTMAS EVE celebration was unlike anything Jane had ever experienced. And all things considered, she felt she'd held it together fairly well. She never lost her temper once. Sure, her smile felt forced at times as she tried to overlook all the disarray and chaos filling her home. She feigned amusement as the grown-ups played charades and the children squealed as they chased each other through the house. She just looked away when food and drink got spilled and carelessly wiped up. And she even sang along when people began to sing carols.

Okay, she bristled as she watched Erik literally throw a bulky log onto the fire in her previously pristine fireplace. Of course, the hearth was now a mess of soot and ash and wood debris. She even tried to look pleased when she observed Olivia and Malcolm setting up a roughly carved nativity set on her marble-top table. Scooting all her graceful Lladró figurines to stand behind their homespun display, the two joked that the fancy angels could watch over the little nativity scene.

Jane had even looked away when she'd spied Malcolm and

Olivia exchanging kisses, rationalizing that of course they would kiss while standing under the ball of mistletoe someone had hung from her foyer chandelier. Even though all her maternal instincts warned her that their relationship was getting serious, that she might very well become related to the McEntires by marriage, she wanted to pretend it was just a neighborly kiss. But she couldn't deny it anymore when she noticed the couple holding hands, gazing at each other with a look that revealed they had moved well beyond just friendly neighbors.

It was in that moment that she knew this was too much. She had tried her best, but she couldn't take another minute of all these festivities. She had reached her boiling point, and she knew she was too tired to control her emotions. The best she could do was make her excuses and apologies. She blamed her aching hip for her early departure, which was partly true, then wheeled herself into the sanctuary of her bedroom.

She closed and locked the door behind her, which only kept out a portion of the noise out there, but still afforded her the privacy she needed to cry. What was wrong with her? Why couldn't she act and react like other people? Was she just so broken that there was no fixing her? She tried to remember the little sermon Rob had given earlier. His words had rung true then. But now it was hard to wrap her head around it. Oh, she could understand the shock Jesus must've felt in coming to a really messy world. She could relate. But he hadn't seemed to mind the mess. He just wanted to be with those messy people, to help those messy people, and, she thought, to perhaps help them clean up their messes.

"I am a mess," she quietly confessed to God as she pulled off her wig. She could only imagine how horrible her short blue hair must look right now, but that wasn't the mess she was referring to. "I need help to clean it up, Lord. *Divine* help." She set the wig on the makeshift stand Cindy had made for her and pulled out a tissue to wipe her running nose. With tears still pouring down her cheeks, she rolled over to her closet, thinking she would attempt to pull off her dress and get ready for bed. Normally Olivia would help her to do this chore, but Jane knew her daughter was preoccupied tonight.

As she sobbed and tugged on the dress, she finally got her head and one arm out but was trapped in the rest of it. Trying to figure a way to remove the dress without standing since her hip was really aching, she caught a glimpse of her image in the full-length mirror on her closet door. Staring at the awkward and slightly shocking image, she realized that she really did look like a mess. A perfect mess.

At first, she gaped at herself in horror, and then realized she looked absolutely, comically, ridiculous. Blue hair sticking out in all directions, red-rimmed eyes, dripping nose, stuck half in and half out of a dress, her underwear exposed and all her wrinkles accentuated by the overhead light. And suddenly, she began to giggle. And then to laugh . . . uncontrollably. And then someone knocked on the bedroom door.

"Mom?" It was Olivia. "May I come in?"

Trying to regain some composure, which was impossible considering everything, Jane wheeled herself over to unlock the door, positioning herself behind it as she opened it a small crack.

"Are you alone?" Jane asked, still suppressing giggles.

"Yes. Do you need help?"

"Do I ever!" She rolled back far enough for Olivia to enter.

"Oh, Mom." Olivia's eyes grew wide. "Are you okay?"

"Well, it depends on how you define *okay*." Jane held up her hands hopelessly. "I'm stuck in this dress, I look perfectly ridiculous, I'm basically a great big mess. But I think I'm okay." She started to giggle.

Olivia bent down to hug her mother. "I'm sorry. I should've come in sooner. But I thought you might've wanted to be alone."

"I thought so too." Jane tried to cooperate as Olivia helped remove her dress. "I used to pride myself on being so independent and self-sufficient. I think God has been trying to teach me that I need people. Not just for getting dressed, but for living life."

"That makes sense."

Jane looked up at her daughter. "I really am trying to get over my perfectionist ways, Olivia, but it's so hard."

"Well, you just said God was showing you that you need people. Maybe you're ready to consider seeing the therapist Pastor Justin mentioned."

Jane nodded. "I think you're right."

Both of them remained quiet as Olivia helped Jane prepare for bed. The ebb and flow of noise from the party still going on out there continued, but it seemed to be a little more subdued, like perhaps they were getting ready to call it a night. Jane thought it was well past the children's bedtimes, but she didn't want to mention it. And then they all began to sing "Silent Night." Jane felt her eyes grow misty.

"Isn't that beautiful," she whispered to Olivia.

Olivia nodded and they both just listened until the song ended, and then, as Olivia helped Jane into bed, it sounded as if people were starting to say their goodbyes and making their departures.

"I was really proud of you tonight," Olivia said as she pulled the comforter up.

"Well, part of it was just a big act."

"That's okay, Mom. Sometimes that's the best we can do. And you know what they say, fake it 'til you make it."

Jane forced a smile. "I'll try to remember that."

"Mom . . ." Olivia sat in the wheelchair next to the bed. "I want to tell you something . . . and I hope it won't upset you."

Jane raised an eyebrow. "About you and Malcolm?"

"You know?"

"I have my suspicions that things are getting serious."

Olivia's face lit up. "Mom, I love him. I really do love him."

Jane pursed her lips, determined not to say the wrong thing, to maybe fake it until she could make it. "And do you think he loves you in the same way?"

"I do, Mom. I really do."

Jane reached for her daughter's hand. "He seems like a fine young man."

"Really? Even though he's a McEntire?"

Jane's smile felt more genuine now. "I'm beginning to see the McEntires in a new light."

"That's what I was hoping for." Olivia bit her lip. "And it's not that I think he's going to—I mean, I'm not trying to rush things—but if Malcolm really does feel like I do, and if he should happen to, well, bring up our future together . . . well, I'd like to think you wouldn't be too opposed to a marriage. I mean, if it comes to that . . . because if he proposes, I'd like to say yes."

Jane sighed. "Well, I must admit that planning a wedding with the McEntires might try my patience, but I would do my best."

Olivia hugged her. “Thank you, Mom. And, really, it’s not like I know this is imminent, but I’d just like to know I had your blessing . . . just in case.”

Jane looked into her daughter’s eyes, and, seeing the sparkle of hope, her heart completely softened toward the young couple. “I really hope you’re right, Olivia. I hope he does propose.”

They hugged again, and then, suspecting Malcolm was out there waiting for Olivia, Jane feigned a yawn and told her daughter goodnight. Olivia turned off the bedside lamp and, as she walked to the door, quietly sang, “I wish you a messy Christmas, I wish you a messy Christmas, I wish you a messy Christmas and a blessed New Year.”

Jane thanked her and chuckled. Then, lying there alone in the dark, she thought, not for the first time, that God really did work in mysterious ways. She silently thanked him for all the messes that had recently come her way, hoping that perhaps they really would pave the way for a blessed new year.

twenty-two

ON CHRISTMAS MORNING, Olivia tried not to focus on the way Malcolm had said goodnight on Christmas Eve. In his defense, things had gotten a little crazy in her house. Some of the younger McEntires had insisted that the older generation, primarily their parents and Olivia's grandmother, call it a night while they lingered in her mom's kitchen to assist with cleanup. And since Malcolm was among the cleanup crew, Olivia had naturally joined in. Everyone was trying to keep it fairly quiet since it was close to midnight, but the general atmosphere continued to be jovial and fun.

Sadie was out of her doggy crate and was running around the kitchen and nearly getting stepped on when Olivia noticed a puddle on the floor right next to the pup. After gently scolding Sadie, like Malcolm had explained was a necessary step in the process of dog training, she grabbed some paper towels and started to clean it up. Meanwhile, Malcolm's youngest brother's new girlfriend scooped up the puppy.

"Poor Sadie," Kristen cooed in baby talk. "Did mean old Olivia yell at you?"

Olivia started to say something, but instead she waited, hoping that Malcolm would come to her defense. But he was too distracted with joking with his sister as they washed dishes, and so she just listened in aggravation as Kristen overblew the whole thing. And then the silly girl walked the pup over to Malcolm.

"Your poor neglected puppy is being growled at," she told him in more baby talk. "Poor little Sadie is in danger of getting stepped on or kicked in here." She sidled up close to him. "Do you want me to take care of her for you, Malcolm? And spare her from this mob?"

He just laughed. "Sure. Thanks. I wouldn't like to see her injured."

"But if she was injured, I bet the big, strong vet could fix the little girl right up." Kristen was clearly flirting now, and maybe Olivia was just tired, but as she tossed the damp paper towel, she was also irritated by the younger girl and her stupid baby talk.

And so she went into the living room, busying herself with straightening things up in there. She knew she was still stewing over Kristen's juvenile behavior, but she'd really hoped that Malcolm would've defended her. Or at least come out to say something to her. After all, she'd simply been doing as he'd told her. She picked a sofa cushion off the floor, plumped it, and set it on the couch.

"Aha," Malcolm said from behind her in a teasing tone. "I found the perfectionist hard at work."

She spun around to face him. "I am *not* a perfectionist."

He looked surprised. "I was just kidding."

She bit her lower lip. "I know. But it's sensitive territory."

"I guess." He frowned slightly. "Sorry."

She thought about explaining herself—that she was only trying to make the house look better in case her mother got up early. After all, she'd already been through a lot, and tomorrow would be another gathering of the Bradshaws and McEntires. Seems like he could appreciate that. But instead, she stood silently.

"I really am sorry," he said. "I didn't mean to step on your toes."

"I think I'm just tired," she told him. *And irritated at Kristen,* she wanted to add, but she knew that would sound childish.

"It's late," he said with a disappointed expression.

"Yeah, tomorrow will be another busy day." She picked up another cushion and tossed it onto the couch. "Guess we should say goodnight."

"Yeah," he agreed. Just then, one of his sisters called out to him to take out the garbage. "Goodnight," he said hastily.

"Goodnight." And despite knowing she was taking this all wrong and acting even more like a baby than silly Kristen, she'd turned and run up the stairs with hot tears burning in her eyes.

But today was a new day, she told herself as she got up early, determined to put a bit more effort into making her mom's house a little tidier. Malcolm could call her a perfectionist if he wanted, but she was simply trying to be considerate. Did she appreciate tidiness and order? Probably . . . but not to the point of perfectionism, she hoped.

As she went into the kitchen, which surprisingly looked better than it had in days, she reminded herself it was Christmas. And it would be a good day. As she made coffee, adding a cinnamon stick to make it festive, she began to hum Christmas carols to herself. Yes, it would be a good day.

She carried her cinnamon-flavored coffee with cream through the house, pausing by the nativity scene Malcolm had carved, and stood there admiring it. Picking up the tiny manger and babe, she felt a sense of wonder. That first Christmas must've been so humble . . . and yet so amazing.

"Good morning," Malcolm quietly said from the landing. "And Merry Christmas." He came down the stairs in stockinged feet, carrying his boots. He set his boots by the front door and then came back to her, slipping an arm around her waist. "Still like it?" he asked, nodding toward the nativity scene.

"Like it?" She smiled at him. "I love it."

"Good. Now I want to apologize for last night." He kissed her forehead. "After you went to bed, my older sister took me aside."

"Jocelyn did?" She peered curiously at him.

"She explained how Kristen was playing you. I should've warned you that Nate's girlfriend is kind of a piece of work. Rumor is he's thinking about breaking up with her."

"Oh?"

"Anyway, Jocelyn explained how Kristen had treated you over Sadie's little accident." He shook his head. "I'm sorry. I guess I missed that. You were doing it exactly right. Kristen is just, well, she's just dumb." He laughed.

"And I guess I was feeling a bit jealous when she was getting all cozy with you."

His eyes lit up. "You were jealous?"

"Yeah, pretty silly, huh?"

He tipped his head to one side. "I don't know. I think it's kind of sweet."

She set down the tiny manger and baby, then looked up at him. "Thanks for apologizing."

He leaned down to kiss her. "Thanks for getting jealous."

She held up her coffee mug, which was now in need of a warm-up. "Want some?"

"I do. But how do you feel about taking a little morning stroll first?" He nodded toward the front window. "It's a clear day, and I'd like to see the sun coming up on the snow."

"Just let me get my coat and boots," she told him.

"Meet me outside."

Olivia's feet felt light as angels' wings as she skipped up the stairs. She had felt confident that last night's little debacle had been mostly in her mind, but it was reassuring to hear Malcolm apologize. And now they would go on a delightful Christmas morning walk. She pulled a knit cap on, slid into her parka, and shoved on her boots, then hurried back downstairs. Malcolm was waiting on the porch.

"Check out that blue sky," he said as they went down the steps. "I just looked at the weather on the other side of the mountain."

"Let me guess. Raining?"

He grinned. "Yep." He took her hand. "I'm not going to miss that."

She wanted to say "Me too" but knew she'd have to explain it.

"Would you ever want to move back here?" he asked as they walked down the footpath, snow crunching underfoot.

"Under the right circumstances, yes."

"What about your job?"

She shrugged. "Fortunately, the kind of work I do can be done off-site. Or if I really wanted, I could get into something else. Sometimes I fantasize about doing something completely different."

"Really?" He paused to look at her. "Like what?"

"I don't know. I mean, I've always been kind of creative. At least, I imagined I was. And when I went to work at the marketing firm, I'd hoped I'd get to exercise some of that creativity. And I suppose I do, but not like I'd hoped."

"What would you do that's more creative?" he asked.

"I'm not sure. Sometimes I imagine having a little craft store. You know, the kind of place where people can come take classes and learn various crafts. Both for kids and adults. I remember how I used to do things like that with your mom. It was always so fun. And this town doesn't really have anything like that anymore."

"That sounds like a great idea. I know my mom would be for it."

"Mine too. I mean, she's always enjoyed crafting. Of course, it was always in her perfectionist way." She chuckled. "Which is exactly why I preferred doing crafts with *your* mom."

They paused by the city park. "Look at that." Malcolm pointed to the gazebo all covered in snow and washed in golden light from the sun now fully coming up.

"Oh my." Olivia gasped. "It's so beautiful. I wish I had my phone to get a picture."

"Take a picture with your brain," he teased. "It lasts longer." He tugged her hand. "Let's go check it out more closely." Leaving a trail of footprints in the freshly fallen snow, they traipsed over to the gazebo, going up the steps and standing inside to look at the eastern horizon now glowing in dawn light. "Merry Christmas," he told her, sealing it with a kiss.

"Merry Christmas," she said back.

"Olivia," he began slowly, his expression suddenly shy. "You may have figured this out by now, but I'd like to say it out loud. I love you."

She felt her throat tighten as she nodded, hoping she'd be able to speak. "I love you too, Malcolm."

His face brightened even more. "How about Sadie?" he asked.

"Sadie?" She felt confused.

"Yeah. Do you love her?"

She laughed. "Of course. I thought you knew that. In fact, I'd like to steal her from you."

"What if we both kept her?"

"Joint custody?" she asked with a tilted head.

And right there in the snow, Malcolm went down on one knee. "Olivia Bradshaw, will you marry me?"

She felt her smile grow wider and wider as she eagerly nodded. "Yes, Malcolm McEntire, I will gladly marry you." Then she fell down to her knees and hugged him.

They exchanged some more enthusiastic kisses until their knees started getting cold, and then he helped her to her feet.

"Do you think the Bradshaws and McEntires can handle this?" he asked. "Particularly your mother?"

"Well, it's already been a pretty messy Christmas for my poor mother," she concluded. "Might as well throw one more happy mess at her."

"Here's to a messy Christmas." He kissed her again.

"A messy Christmas to you too." She laughed.

The End

Melody Carlson is the award-winning author of more than 250 books with sales of more than 7.5 million, including many bestselling Christmas novellas, young adult titles, and contemporary romances. She has received a *Romantic Times* Career Achievement Award, her novel *All Summer Long* has been made into a Hallmark movie, and the movie based on her novel *The Happy Camper* premiered on UPtv in 2023. She and her family live in central Oregon.